Homecoming

AT CRESCENT LAKE HIGH SCHOOL

MATT SMITH

NORTH STATE STREET PUBLISHING | ANN ARBOR, MICH

North State Street Publishing | Ann Arbor, Michigan, USA

ENGLISH

1	A	B	C	D	21	A	B	C	D	41	A	B		
2	F	G	H	J	22	F	G	H	J	42	F	G		
3	A	B	C	D	23	A	B	C	D	43	A	B		
4	F	G	H	J	24	F	G	H	J	44	F	G		
5	A	B	C	D	25	A	B	C	D	45	A	B		
6	F	G	H	J	26	F	G	H	J	46	F	G		
7	A	B	C	D	27	A	B	C	D	47	A	B		
8	F	G	H	J	28	F	G	H	J	48	F	G		
9	A	B	C	D	29	A	B	C	D	49	A	B		
10	F	G	H	J	30	F	G	H	J	50	F	G		
11	A	B	C	D	31	A	B	C	D	51	A	B		
12	F	G	H	J	32	F	G	H	J	52	F	G		
13	A	B	C	D	33	A	B	C	D	53	A	B		
14	F	G	H	J	34	F	G	H	J	54	F	G		
15	A	B	C	D	35	A	B	C	D	55	A	B		
16	F	G	H	J	36	F	G	H	J	56	F	G		
17	A	B	C	D	37	A	B	C	D	57	A	B		
18	F	G	H	J	38	F	G	H	J	58	F	G		
19	A	B	C	D	39	A	B	C	D	59	A	B		
20	F	G	H	J	40	F	G	H	J	60	F	G		

MATHEMATICS

1	A	B	C	D	E	16	F	G	H	J	K	31	A	
2	F	G	H	J	K	17	A	B	C	D	E	32	F	
3	A	B	C	D	E	18	F	G	H	J	K	33	A	
4	F	G	H	J	K	19	A	B	C	D	E	34	F	
5	A	B	C	D	E	20	F	G	H	J	K	35	A	
6	F	G	H	J	K	21	A	B	C	D	E	36	F	
7	A	B	C	D	E	22	F	G	H	J	K	37	A	
8	F	G	H	J	K	23	A	B	C	D	E	38	F	
9	A	B	C	D	E	24	F	G	H	J	K	39	A	
10	F	G	H	J	K	25	A	B	C	D	E	40	F	
11	A	B	C	D	E	26	F	G	H	J	K	41	A	
12	F	G	H	J	K	27	A	B	C	D	E	42	F	
13	A	B	C	D	E	28	F	G	H	J	K	43	A	
14	F	G	H	J	K	29	A	B	C	D	E	44	F	
15	A	B	C	D	E	30	F	G	H	J	K	45	A	

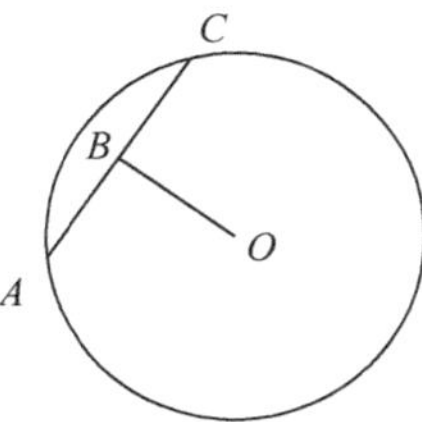

Note: Figure not drawn to scale.

1. Beatus qui legit et qui audiunt verba prophetiae et servant ea quae in scripta sunt tempus enim prope est.

   A.   3
   B. $3\sqrt{2}$
   C. $3\sqrt{3}$
   D.   6
   E. $6\sqrt{3}$

There were 41 hours, 11 minutes, and 05 seconds until 7:27am Sunday morning on the otherwise unremarkable Friday afternoon when class let out at Crescent Lake High School. Michael didn't stop to count. He wasn't thinking about it. Why would he? He wouldn't even know the horrible significance of 7:27am Sunday morning for another 31 hours anyway.

The last bell had just rung, indicating the end of the last period of the last day of Homecoming Week at Crescent Lake. There was a football game scheduled for that evening and a semi-formal dance Saturday night. Michael was fighting his way against the steady stream of student traffic headed the opposite direction down the hallway. The currents were always running against him, it seemed.

Just moments before, he was sitting in his 6th period General Chemistry class having a sex fantasy about his lab partner and ancient crush, a recently-turned seventeen-year-old brunette girl-next-door named Emmaleigh. At the beginning of the semester, Michael had silently prayed that he would draw her from the random seating assignment as his lab partner, and when the teacher did indeed seat them together he accepted it as one of the few signs of the existence of a gentle, loving God.

The teacher stood at the board, his back to the classroom, fumbling the pages of his textbook and scratching his head, floundering ineptly in an attempt to teach himself the difference between ionic and covalent bonds before teaching it to his students. He had long since achieved tenure, but that was no reason to rest on his laurels.

Michael wouldn't have learned the lesson anyway. He was preoccupied by remembering the way Emmaleigh was dressed during the National Honor Society initiation ceremony the previous spring. She was a modest dresser, but on this particular night she happened to wear a low cut blouse that revealed the slightest suggestion of her cleavage, which was made all the more alluring by the fact that she had theretofore and thereafter kept it so concealed. She wore a smart black skirt that rose above the knee and wore sheer black stockings that had a very subtle geometric pattern, accentuating every curve down to her heels.

Michael imagined her kicking those heels off onto her bedroom floor at home, while she curled on her bed with her chemistry homework.

The doorbell would ring.

She would bound down the stairs to answer it, her
skirt, falling precisely 3½" above the knee and
therefore a lewd violation of the dress code, bouncing
in stride.

He would be on the front porch.

She would throw open the door to reveal him.

"I'm here for our study group," he would say.

"My parents are out of town," she would respond for
some reason. "And I took the cover off of the hot tub."

He would coolly accept the invitation.

She would lead him out to the tub under a starry
sky; they would both strip down to their underwear and
slip into the water; her leg would meet his; he would
look deeply into her blue eyes and paralyze her with
his coolness; they would tacitly abandon pretense and
kiss ferociously, like failing levees; his hand,
meanwhile, would find her leg, run up her calf, along
her thigh--

And that's where the fantasy would abruptly stop.

It simply wasn't plausible. If it were her house,
why would she need to go in the tub in her underwear?
Surely she would have a swimsuit somewhere. Far more
problematic was the biological problem: what happens
when his hand reaches the northern terminus of her leg?
His experience with vaginas was purely academic,
limited to an awkward, blushing evasion of a lesson
about its biological function that was taught in his
10th grade health class. And besides, even had he a
sufficient knowledge of the female anatomy, the least
plausible aspect of his hot tub rendezvous is that
Michael could ever be that smooth. In real life he

would probably stammer and say something stupid, like
"I've always found Taco Bell hot sauce to be hotter
than Taco Bell fire sauce, even though it is supposed
to be the reverse," or "Even though I was never in Boy
Scouts, I've always been very good at tying knots." The
veracity of both statements notwithstanding, they are
not phrases that get one invited to hot tub parties in
underwear, even imagined ones.

And ultimately... there was that note.

Several weeks ago he had attempted to summon the
courage to talk to her about his pining, but when he
gained her audience, he couldn't articulate anything
useful.

So he did the worst thing possible: he committed it
to writing. On wide-ruled paper, of all curious choices
of media. "Dear Emmaleigh," his horrible note started,
prosaically, "Since the first day I ever saw you..."
and from there it quickly trailed off from the banal to
the tedious. When she asked to borrow his lab notes on
limiting reactants, he surreptitiously slipped the love
letter among them. Immediately he realized how pathetic
it was:

"I got your note," she would NEVER say, "and it made
me realize that I need you inside me and also a
passionate, concomitant courtship."

But he had sent it anyway, and his instant regret
was a force too impotent to retrieve it. Michael hoped
that if he concentrated very hard the letter would
spontaneously combust.

Fortunately, this was two weeks ago and she had
never brought it up. Perhaps she didn't study off of

his notes and find his pathetic tell-all. Or perhaps it had fallen into the toilet while she was peeing at school, sucked to Hades by one of those vicious automatic-flush toilets that were known to fire autonomously and without warning thrice per excretion, and afterward she was too embarrassed to tell him what happened. Sure, that could be it, he would comfort himself, before trying to erase the shame that he enjoyed thinking about Emmaleigh jumping up from a semi-sentient automatic-flush toilet set on consuming her.

Students continued to collide with him as he made his way down the hall toward his locker. He was finally intercepted by his best friend, Kody, who loved him dearly but had an agenda.

"Did you do it yet?" he asked eagerly.

"Do what?" replied Michael, though he knew what Kody was getting at.

"The Homecoming dance is tomorrow night. You have about thirty-five seconds left to find a date."

"Yeah, I was actually--"

"Thirty-four!" Kody interrupted him with a countdown timer, ignoring what was sure to be an inexcusable cop-out.

"--just going to stay at home. I'm like--"

"Thirty-three!"

"Shut up! I'm like super close to unlocking All Guns on Goldeneye."

Kody made a gagging sound to register his disappointment in his friend. "First, that's lame.

You're lame." Michael shrugged. He had made peace with himself about that. "Second," Kody added, exposing the lie, "you already did that. You called me afterward, remember? It was like two weeks ago."

Oh right. "Okay, fine, then I have to..." Michael tried to come up with another excuse. "Screw it," he concluded, "I'm just not going. Quit asking."

"C'mon. There are still girls out there who are dateless. Like Megyn Fitzsimmons?"

"Megyn and I are friends," rebutted Michael. "And I respect her too much to make her go on a date with me."

Kody rolled his eyes. "Okay, fine," he conceded, attempting a different tack. "But not all girls want to be respected, Mike. Like Reghan Weaver for instance," he said, elbowing him, "who also doesn't have a date."

Michael scoffed. "Reghan Weaver is the easiest girl at Crescent Lake High School."

"Exactly!" said Kody. "That's why you've got to strike while the iron's hot! A sure thing can't stay dateless for long."

And there it was.

"Is that what this is about?" asked Michael. "Why are you so concerned about me getting laid?"

"I just want to help a brother out, that's all."

"Get over yourself. You've had sex like, what, one time? Practically on accident? Now you're trying to lead us sad virgins out of the..., uh..." he struggled and trailed off while fumbling the metaphor. "Like Roaul Wallenberg," he said in an unintelligible mutter.

Kody narrowed his eyes and shook his head.

Michael grunted. "The point is, eat shit. Leave me alone."

"Mike," Kody said with the urgency of an orthopedic surgeon selling elective surgery, "You've got to score."

"Shut up, you ass. Besides, who says I'm interested in just 'scoring'? Maybe I'm interested in..." Michael started to trail off and slowed his walking pace, looking across the crowded hallway that suddenly seemed very intimate. "Maybe I'm interested in more than that," he finished.

Kody followed his gaze to Emmaleigh's locker, where she was packing up textbooks and some kind of hand lotion she had purchased at the mall rather than at the grocery.

"You're pathetic," he said.

"Totidem verbis," Michael agreed. Kody didn't understand the phrase. But rather than ask him to translate he decided to press the issue.

"You've had a thing for Emmaleigh since the ninth grade. Why don't you just ask her out already?"

"I will," replied Michael. "I'm just waiting for the right moment."

"When, graduation?"

Michael frowned. "Ten-year class reunion at the latest, I swear."

They continued down the hall. Michael tried to be cool and nonchalant at the same time. Maybe if he walked perfectly cool and nonchalantly, she would notice how cool and nonchalant he was and would be effected to offer that elusive invitation to the hot tub. But Kody sabotaged him.

"Tell you what. About this 'right moment' you're waiting for?"

"Yeah?"

"It's here," Kody announced as he shoved Michael violently across three freshmen and into Emmaleigh's locker.

Michael landed on his head. The locker reverberated like a crash cymbal.

"Oh my God," exclaimed Emmaleigh. "Are you okay?"

"Yeah," Michael replied, standing coolly and nonchalantly. "I'm just... intense I guess." He rolled his own eyes at himself.

Kody gave Michael a big thumbs-up. Michael returned a very subtle middle finger that Emmaleigh didn't notice.

A moment of uninspired silence occurred. It was awkward. Emmaleigh was too polite to let it continue.

"Good luck at the game tonight. I'll be cheering for you." Michael thought too hard about the statement. He was good at that. She'll be cheering for me? Me specifically? Maybe she's just being nice. She was very good at being nice. Or maybe she was being equivocal. Michael couldn't tell when girls were being either, and with Emmaleigh he certainly wouldn't be able to tell. He was born with two singular traits: one of them rendered him completely unable to discern from otherwise unsubtle cues whether a girl was interested or uninterested in him.

The other is far more consequential, and the impetus for the coming ordeal.

Michael's terminal awkwardness, however, did not deter the efforts of those who didn't yet know him well. Indeed one terrible night the week before school started again, he was at the party of a friend-of-a-friend who attended a different school and had foreign, alien, from-another-school people there. There he caught the attention of an otherwise charming co-ed who had endured his benign, stilted conversation because she thought he was acceptably handsome and was disarmed by his inimitable clumsiness. Sometime before midnight she had snared him into a darkened room, whereupon the violent necking escalated into her expectation for sex. Michael froze. "I can't," he said, improvising an excuse that was designed to remove him from the situation without hurting her feelings. "I have a venereal disease."

"Oh my God," said the would-be paramour, "which one?"

When he couldn't immediately summon an acceptable malady he simply shrugged and responded, "All of them," and hastened to add, "Especially the worst ones."

She looked at him inquisitively for only a moment before his guilt compelled him to confess to the lie, stammering:

"I don't have a venereal disease.

"I'm sorry.

"I don't know why I said that."

The mood having been sadly asphyxiated, she lost interest and wandered off and later that night violently thrashed the queen mattress in the out-of-town parents' guest room with some other senior boy who was flying off the three light beers and shot of Parrot Bay that he had drank earlier that night, even though he was less attractive than Michael and had scored two entire standard deviations lower on the ACT last April.

"Thanks," said Michael to Emmaleigh. He followed it up with another awkward moment of silence. This time she couldn't rescue him from himself. "Okay," he concluded. "Good talk. I'll see you later." He took a step away, but somehow gathered the courage to breach it.

"Actually, hey," he said, returning, "Did you get a chance to look through those chem notes I gave you last Friday?"

Emmaleigh averted her eyes back to her locker. "No, not yet. Sorry. I've been really busy."

"Oh, good," said Michael, relieved, but he quickly caught himself. "I mean, that's cool. I was just... Look, I was wondering... I know it's last minute and everything, but... I was curious if..."

She interrupted him. "Are you going to the Homecoming dance tomorrow?"

He was surprised at the convenient segue. Why was she bringing this up? Was she hoping for an invitation from him?

"Well, actually..."

"Because if you are," she said, "then I'll see you there. Cayden McCaffrey asked me to be his date yesterday."

Michael felt that thing that happens in a Scorcese movie when they zoom in and dolly out at the same time.

"Michael," said Emmaleigh, "Are you okay?"

He looked at her with the charm of one who has suffered a closed-head injury. "Cayden McCaffrey?" he repeated, "Yesterday?" He started shaking his head and repeating, "That's great. Great. Great."

Emmaleigh looked at him blankly.

"Great."

He snapped-to after a moment and attempted to salvage some shred of dignity. "Anyways," he said, "I was just about to say that I was curious if you knew what time it is?"

She gestured to an enormous clock with blazing red digital numbers that was mounted not 25 feet behind her.

"Great," said Michael.

A geological era of awkwardness passed.

There were 41 hours, 02 minutes, and 31 seconds until 7:27am Sunday morning.

"So then I just stood there, nodding my head and looking like an idiot," he explained to Kody. It was late in the 4th quarter and Michael still wore a pristine blue jersey that had not yet seen the field. Kody's had grass stains from his service on kick-return duty and the one play he subbed-in for Jaxson Turner, who was thought to be concussed but was merely slowed by the indigestion that followed his pregame meal of a bag of 3-D Doritos.

"Back at square zero it seems," Kody ruminated.

"It doesn't make a difference. You know she's going with Cayden McCaffrey?"

"Yeah," said Kody impatiently. "You told me. Like six times every hour for the last two hours. You're like the Weather Channel of the social lives of people I don't care about."

"It doesn't make any sense," Michael said aloud, more to himself than Kody. "What's she see in him anyway?"

Kody tilted his head. "Are we talking about the same Cayden McCaffrey?"

At this exact moment, the hero in question commanded the huddle on the field, a leader among leaders, cooler than cool.

Cayden McCaffrey was difficult to not like, and an attempt to make him an adversary was not an easy one. As the quarterback and team captain, he was revered among his teammates and had something reaffirming to say to each, even those who saw little playing time. Among opponents, he was magnanimous in both victory and defeat. Even the sorest loser on the opposing sideline recognized and appreciated his talent, evident on the field and well-documented in the provincial newspaper of their small media market. Universities within the census-designated region pursued him with either full-scholarships or preferred walk-on status. He never turned down an invitation to a party but usually passed when offered a beer, instead serving as a designated driver whenever someone needed to sneak in before curfew. He held a 3.4 GPA, which wouldn't get him into the Ivys but, in the aggregate of his other talents, would take him to whichever state school he wanted to attend.

His congeniality and personality had compelled his peers to push him into student government despite his modest reluctance to run. He agreed on the condition that he wasn't put up for president or any other contested position. He didn't want to have to compete against a classmate in what typically amounted to a popularity contest, a superficial reaffirmation for the winner and an ego-bruise for the loser. He was disaffected by the subjective nature of these elections and accepted a nomination for treasurer because the contest was unopposed. It would require his partisans to hang no posters that touted his virtues over his hypothetical opponent's inadequacies. A single vote would have put him in the position; nevertheless he still earned more than 99% of those who cast ballots the previous spring. His unanimous election was sabotaged by some Guy Fawkes who had written-in Alexander Hamilton as an ironic protest of the fatuous concept of student government. Cayden wasn't offended by it. Besides, by the end of the football season, he'd be a unanimous coaches' pick for Division II first-team All State, and that was a more flattering caucus.

"A better question," Kody said to Michael on the lonely bench, "is what's Cayden see in her? No offense man, but she's a total prude. Cold like February. Third base with her would probably give you frostbite." Kody pantomimed his fingers falling off and the subsequent terror of it.

Michael didn't respond. He was staring off into the distance. This was not unusual for him.

"No action there, you know," Kody continued. When Michael didn't reply, Kody repeated himself. "No action

there," he said again, poking his tongue in his cheek
to intimate fellacio. Again, Michael didn't notice.

"Do you see this?" Michael asked.

"What?"

"This cheerleader over there." Michael pointed very
subtly toward a dark-haired girl on the visitor's
sideline.

Kody squinted. "Which one?"

"On the far left. Front row."

"What about her?" asked Kody.

"She's trying to get my attention."

Kody appraised her as a female specimen and
concluded Michael was wrong.

"Maybe you've got something on your face."

"No, seriously," Michael said. "I swear, she just
waved at me. She's been doing it all night. At first I
thought I was seeing things but I'm not."

"Hey, remember that one time at lunch last spring
when you thought the janitor was staring at you?"

"He was. It was creepy."

Kody returned his attention to the line of
scrimmage. The squad was down three points and the game
clock ticked underneath a minute. The contest was too
much in peril to bother with his nonsense. "I think you
have a psychosis," he said, dismissing him.

"She just did it again!" Michael snapped.

"She's like 60 yards away!" Kody rebutted. "She
could be waving at anyone."

Michael frowned.

Kody continued. "She's probably waving at Cayden McCaffrey." He smiled and turned the knife. "Don't you know? All the girls want to bone him."

Michael fumed, shifted on the bench, and turned back to view the stands. He focused on Emmaleigh, whom he had located well before the kickoff as the marching band was unintentionally dishonoring the school & the community & the alumni with its performance of the school song.

She waved a blue & white pompon with enchanting grace. She seemed to do it in slow motion. The stadium flood lights illuminated her more generously than they did the remainder of the student body. Something heroic erupted inside him.

Michael turned to the score board.

His squad was down 20-17.

0:41 seconds left on the game clock.

35 yards from the end zone.

Head Coach called his last timeout and pulled his offense into a huddle. Michael rose from the bench with intent and resolve.

"Hey, where are you going?" asked Kody, but his question went unanswered. Michael bullied his way into the huddle with his own call.

"Coach, put me in," Michael demanded. "Let's run Strong Thirty-two Smoke."

Everyone looked at Michael as though he had just suffered a closed-head injury. It was a deceptive trick play that, if executed correctly, would have Michael scoring the go-ahead touchdown on a long pass from Cayden. If executed wrong, in this circumstance, the game would be over and the Homecoming effort ignominiously ruined. It was, like many of Michael's ideas, a quixotic risk.

"Get out of the huddle," responded Head Coach.

"They'll never expect it!" Michael protested.

"We've got to get you a tighter helmet," opined an assistant coach who had risen meteorically to his position after knocking up his girlfriend during his second semester at community college. The rest of the players indicated accord.

But then an unlikely ally chimed in.

"Coach, let's do it." The advocate was Cayden McCaffrey himself. Michael felt uneasy. This made it more difficult to hate him. "It'll work," Cayden continued. "And Michael's faster than anyone on the field." It was true; Michael was exceptionally fast. The previous spring he had won the 400 meter dash at the conference track meet. Friends on the squad joked that he had developed his speed to escape girls who asked for his phone number.

The members of the huddle, however, with the game in jeopardy, exchanged tacit glances.

But if Cayden said so...

Head Coach relented on the endorsement of his teenage superstar and Michael took the field. Ten athletes in visiting whites lined up against the heroes in blue at scrimmage. Michael lined up far from them. A single white jersey floated out toward Michael, the opponent skeptical that Michael's otherwise unimpressive frame would be of consequence.

Cayden snapped the ball and the line collapsed on the decoy as planned. Michael meanwhile took one quick shuffle off the line and broke down the field, leaving the skeptical adversary with a gaped jaw and a life lesson about appraising talent. After only a few yards, he cut a slant toward the goalpost. And just as only he and Cayden had predicted, he was wide open on the field. All alone. Poised for greatness.

Cayden threw a perfect spiral in a perfect trajectory that would find its target in perfect stride. His passes, like his smile and even his penmanship, were always perfect. Michael extended his arms to snag the football. But just as it was about to fall into his numbers, he caught in his peripheral vision that very same cheerleader who was making suggestive gestures to him all night.

She blew him a kiss; Michael did a fatal double take.

There were 35 hours, 24 minutes until Sunday's dawn and a mere 0:34 seconds left on the game clock when Michael, distracted by the cheerleader, dropped the game-winning pass.

The players returned to the locker room, the sting
of sabotage evident on their faces. No one but Kody
would even make eye contact with the saboteur. "I guess
we know why that cheerleader was waving at you," said
Kody.

Michael shrugged a conciliatory shrug.

Cayden walked up to him and gave him a pat on the
back. "Don't sweat it. It was a good gamble. We'll get
it next time." Yes, it was very, very difficult to hate
him.

Few of the players showered in the locker room after
the games, reluctant to put themselves on display.
There was too much at risk. What if the water were too
cold? What if they were to find themselves in the
pitied 29.2% of that cruel normal distribution?

One of the fullbacks always did, though. He knew he was hung. When he shampooed his hair he did it with both hands and in a wide stance, the way Gene Kelly might have done it if he ever did a full-frontal musical scene.

Cayden did not have the insecurities that the rest of the team did. He showered to clean off the contest, not to impress, intimidate, or build himself taller by standing next to someone shorter. He was comfortable with himself to a degree that was unusual among seventeen-year-olds.

The stalls were empty when he dropped his towel and turned on the spigot. When he turned around to let the water run down his back, he was alarmed to see a strange man locked on him with keen interest.

Cayden quickly shut off the water and robed himself.

"Can I help you?" he asked in a tone that was not particularly obliging.

"You're a very talented quarterback, Mr. McCaffrey. Do you know where you're playing next year?"

Cayden paused with skepticism. "Is this an interview? Because usually we do this on the field, where I have clothes on."

The stranger smirked. "Where are you playing?" He turned a business card in his fingers. Cayden didn't notice that both sides were blank.

He relented for some reason and acceded to the interview. "I don't know yet. The offers are still coming in."

"Any good ones?"

"A few Division I-As," Cayden replied.

The stranger breathed in and exhaled slowly. "Where do you want to play?" he asked.

"If I could play anywhere?" He paused for a moment, somewhat embarrassed by the magnitude of his immodest aspirations. "U.C.L.A. Definitely." He smiled. He had, for quite some time, daydreamed of playing the Rose Bowl every other Saturday.

"What a coincidence," said the stranger.

He passed the blank card to Cayden, except now it read:

John Smith

Skill Coach - Department of Athletics

University of California, Los Angeles

Cayden refused to believe it. "Are you serious?"

"Our other quarterback flipped."

"This isn't real."

"You'd be number 25. The last spot on the signing roster. The only thing is, the offer expires tonight."

Cayden couldn't believe it. This was too good to be true. The scout unrolled a letter-of-intent that concealed a significant amount of fine print. Cayden hesitated.

Much later that night, Michael, for reasons he couldn't really explain, decided that he would attend the dance. He went to his closet and found a striped tie and knotted it with surprising precision into an impressive full-Windsor knot. He uncinched it and hung it on a rack in his closet.

His title was Night/Weekend Custodian but he was often working overtime. His name was Gabriel. Students had seen him before and dismissed him as strange.

And sure enough, here he was at the school on Saturday morning at 02:15 ante meridiem. In the girls' bathroom. Going through the little boxes mounted in the stalls intended for feminine refuse.

One by one he opened and attempted to empty the boxes. Yet he was increasingly troubled: they were all empty.

The entire female student body was off their periods. Fecund soil for nightshade.

Yes, this was troubling indeed.

"It's happening," Gabriel said to himself. "Tonight's the night." He took a slow, deep breath. His timecard would remain unpunched.

What might potentially be the last sunrise to ever occur over Crescent Lake High School began at 07:26am on Saturday morning. Mackenzie Miller and McKenzie Simon were there only a few hours later to lead the Spirit Committee, comprised of a dozen volunteers eager to add the activity to their college resumes, to supervise the construction of the ceremony, glitter, and shininess.

The Homecoming dance would take place in the fieldhouse, a magnificent structure added onto the building only recently to accommodate the multifarious activities of the athletic body of Crescent Lake High School. The school also had a complete, conventional gymnasium where only three years ago the varsity basketball and volleyball teams played their heroic seasons, including a thrilling district championship in boys' basketball.

The new fieldhouse, however, featured more bleachers and better accessibility, brighter lights & prettier hardwood & shinier silk banners. And since the school now had two regulation basketball & volleyball courts, the school would find less in-fighting for practice time between its multiple athletic squads. But most importantly, the addition provided the requisite capacity to host district and state tournaments that would bring local & regional prestige in addition to the accompanying ticket income. Visitors would leave in both humiliated defeat and suppressed envy as they exited the handsome space, colored in the school livery of blue and silver, an intertwined "CL" logo at center court and "Lakers" painted at either end of the lacquered hardwood surface.

The court itself was transformed into a makeshift dance floor, a DJ set up at the far end on a small elevated stage, and about two dozen round cafeteria tables draped with silver vinyl tablecloths, a handful of glitter tossed across them and blue & silver balloons rising from their centers. The bleachers had been pushed into the wall, revealing the "CLHS" painted in six-foot letters across them. Stairs rose from the side of the court to a second-level mezzanine, which accessed the four-lane track that ran the perimeter of the fieldhouse and additional bleachers that served as the nosebleeds in the modest Division II sized arena. McKenzie led a crew of volunteers around the track, mounting glittered foamcore stars with velcro adhesive

tape and tying the final three-dozen blue & silver
balloons in perfectly equidistant segments along the
railing that overlooked the court.

"Hey you!" she called to a sophomore girl on the
other side of the mezzanine who probably wouldn't
volunteer next year and would just do yearbook instead.
"Move those about two feet to your left!"

At 07:31pm the sun set over Crescent Lake High
School. The DJ sound-checked his monitors, speakers,
and microphones. Elsewhere, in the janitorial shop,
Gabriel the Janitor drew a solid red line in permanent
marker on the face of his analog wall clock somewhere
between the numerals that marked the 15 and 20 minute
marks. He stepped back and studied it uneasily.

In 29 minutes the doors would open; the dance was
scheduled to end at 11:30pm.

It wouldn't.

For lack of better diversions in the community, the unknowingly cursed, veritably doomed student body arrived fashionably on-time. They arrived in their beater cars that they financed with their own summer jobs or their parents' new leases that they vacuumed and hand-washed earlier in the day or their families' nostalgic classics that were tarped in winter and only insured through the summer months. Six even arrived in a limousine, though most eschewed the chauffeured rides until prom, when the vehicles would better match their rented tuxedos & evening ties & chilled salad forks that would be used during the wrong course anyway.

The arriving students were welcomed by four chaperones in the large main entryway under the flagpole that auspiciously flew at full-mast. All four were distinguished members of the faculty, readily willing (though two with feigned protest) to volunteer for the evening for various ulterior reasons.

Mrs. Fuchs was a late forty-something who probably looked pretty good back in her college sorority days and whose passenger manifest of partners probably went well beyond Mr. Fuchs. She now taught the Home Economics and Health classes; the former was an elective but the latter was required for all students in the tenth grade. Though the two courses were distinct, they shared alarmingly significant portions of their respective syllabi.

Señora Carroll, an indisputable Caucasian, taught Spanish I through IV, coached the JV volleyball team in winters, and had probably recently summited the age of 30. Principal Strong was generally friendly and accessible but austere when the situation demanded it. The Spanish teacher and the Principal seemed to share very few things in common, save for that they both drove domestic automobiles and were both married to other people and were both rumored by some in the faculty lounge to be carrying on an illicit romance with each other.

Ms. Fulmer was a 22-year-old student teacher whose emphasis was English Literature. Crescent Lake's proximity to a major teaching college made it a frequent station for fourth-year undergrads learning their vocations by fire. Just as she looked daily in class, so too tonight she was uninterested & disengaged. For someone with a proficient knowledge of the Romantics, she often looked bored and uninspired. Her listlessness, however, did not prevent dozens of her male students from fantasizing about after-hours lessons with her, and her benign salutation of "Ms."

somehow only emphasized rather than concealed her
potential availability.

Mrs. Fuchs was not advertising it but had dozens of
prophylactics on her person. She figured that a few
students were going to do it anyway, and it was better
to help them stay safe. If she could find a way to
coach them through it, all the better. Principal Strong
suspected her roguery but appreciated her attempt at
subterfuge. He was too tired of fighting with her about
it, himself a proxy for outraged parents who thought
her curriculum was, ahem, too comprehensive.

She greeted the couples known to be items. "How are
you, XY and XX? Nice tie. Great dress." She had hoped
to divine some information from their responses that
might indicate whether they were "active," and, more
importantly, whether they were enjoying it. Perhaps her
presence was only going to exacerbate things on this
particularly cursed night.

No one greeted Michael as he entered the building in
a slow, cautious manner, treading as if he had never
been there before and unsure why he changed his mind
about attending. He was fashionably late, but not
intentionally. He had walked out of the house in
slacks, shirt & tie, jacket, and, by thoughtless force
of routine, his old running shoes that he wore to
school every day. When he realized he was in the wrong
pair, he was already halfway to the school. He
deliberated for a few minutes over whether to go back
and retrieve his dress pair. Screw it, he finally
decided. Who would even notice?

Upon arrival, he attempted to casually reconnoiter his surroundings to try to identify anyone within his circle of friends or, even better, Emmaleigh. With any luck, her terrible, horrible, well-liked & affable date would be elsewhere, surrounded by adoring sycophants, leaving her cruelly abandoned & alone & uncomfortable, whereupon Michael could rescue her and they could build some confederate romance upon their shared feelings of being so coincidentally alone and insecure. Until that moment, however, he feigned poise. He adjusted the knot in his tie and gently ran his right hand through his hair, trying to reinforce the part he had put in it, but actually mussing it by a slight degree.

It was then that he received his first salutation of an evening that would prove to have too many.

"Michael! You suck!" exclaimed a freshman whom Michael had never met before. Their disparate class ranks made this a significant dressing-down.

He shrugged in partial accord.

En route to the fieldhouse, Michael passed through the commons area, an open, spacious room that served multiple utility purposes beyond its primary function of lunchtime dining. It was bordered on one side by two enormous walk-in trophy cases that overflowed with dozens of trophies and plaques from conference championships and various athletic contests that had accumulated over the years, including the six state championship trophies that the school had annexed since 1940. Also included were various memorabilia from the ancient advent of the community school: black & white

photos, old letterman sweaters, historic class rings
that looked identical to the ones still sold every
spring. It was a backdrop that, with Michael juxtaposed
against it, only emphasized his recent athletic
misadventure and failed contribution to the school's
glorious legacy.

He entered the fieldhouse like a free radical,
aimless, absorbing the intricate & impressive way that
the court had been transformed by the balloons & muted
light & glitter, and was suddenly stung by his own
conspicuous datelessness. A cursory glance around the
room suggested that everyone in the building --
literally everyone -- was paired up, in the company of
a date whose corsage or tie complemented its mate like
contiguous puzzle pieces, forming a scene into which he
did not fit. Cool looking freshmen were paired up.
Awkward juniors were paired up. Even Churchy Girl, a
fellow senior with a reputation for puritan values,
stood too close to a date, some guy whose hair, dress,
and disposition suggested he had already earned his
high school diploma. It was always kind of strange to
see old guys come back to the school dances. What
cooler adult things were they forfeiting, or perhaps
ostracized from, in order to be at the high school, in
the company of minors?

The DJ was playing party tracks from his milk crates
of compact discs, but it was too early for most of the
students to brave the dance floor. Most lingered near
tables, socializing, discussing their fancy dinners
that they had ordered earlier that evening in
restaurants with cloth napkins, the ceremony of it made

all the more cosmopolitan by the fact they wore ties and dresses into those restaurants.

Mackenzie Miller found him first. "There you are!" she fumed. Michael turned toward her. "You're not allowed to bring a date from another school without getting permission from the Spirit Committee," she lambasted.

Though she was making direct eye contact with Michael, there was no way she was talking to him, because she was describing someone else. Someone with not only the potential to attract a date, but also the ability to recruit from outside his own geography. He turned around to see who was standing behind him, trying to identify the sad, humiliated person whom Mackenzie was dressing down.

But there was no one there. He realized she could only be addressing him.

"Uh, what?" rebutted Michael in powerful rhetoric that rivaled Cicero.

"That girl you're with tonight. She said her name was Lucy or something?"

"...Me?"

"Yes, you!" she said, exhausting the little patience she already had for the kid who had ruined the Homecoming game and was already on the precipice of ruining the Homecoming dance by opening the door to foreign interlopers.

"She's not allowed to be here," said Mackenzie sternly.

"I agree," Michael said deferentially. "I didn't invite a 'Lucy or something'," he professed. "I don't have a date from here or anywhere else."

"Well she said you invited her," Mackenzie replied, ignoring his appeal, preferring the comfort of her own righteous outrage.

"I didn't," Michael said firmly to no one, as Mackenzie had already turned on her heel to fume and issue citations elsewhere.

Michael muttered to himself, annoyed but not surprised that he could find himself dateless, rejected by his true love & the world at large, but still somehow culpable for an uninvited companion.

Having been at the dance for only ten minutes and already twice assailed for crimes both real and pretended, he finally saw an ally and made his way toward him.

Kody and Jordyn were among the paired couples. They stood close together, both of Jordyn's hands on her date, not in any lewd manner but rather in a somewhat possessive way, unable or unwilling to release her boyfriend into the world for fear he might wander off like a lost dog. Kody didn't mind. The closeness of a girl was still novel to him.

She wore some teal-ish kind of spaghetti-strapped dress, and he wore some kind of argyle tie with blue and green hues that were made more adorably obvious when he stood adjacent to her. Whether the color-coordination was deliberate or coincidental, Michael didn't know and preferred not to learn.

"You guys should take that to the chemical shower," he interrupted. "Cool off a bit."

Jordyn sighed and turned to Kody, completing a thought that might have had something to do with her boyfriend's best friend.

"...and that's why," she said to Kody, completing an argument she had started earlier. She looked back at Michael as if she were looking at one of those little micro-goombas from Mario Brothers 3 that prevent your guy from jumping. Kody looked at his friend sadly & sympathetically, as if he were charged with locking a puppy in a kennel for a few hours. Michael didn't seem to infer the nature of either of their looks and bullied through them.

"Hey, did you guys hear anything about my date?" asked Michael.

"You brought a date?" asked Jordyn and Kody at the same time, both of their tones indicating surprise, even shock.

"No," said Michael. "I don't think so."

There was a confused pause as Jordyn and Kody both tried to solve his Who's-On-First puzzle.

"Then why would you ask?" asked Kody.

"I don't know," answered Michael, inspiring little confidence.

Jordyn exchanged a glance with Kody that he interpreted correctly. Fortunately, Michael noticed someone else across the room, and Kody was spared the indignity of sending his friend away.

Michael pardoned himself from Kody & Jordyn's company without doing either of them the courtesy of a

fully formed excuse. "Guys, I've got to, uh...
Something else." Neither Kody nor Jordyn minded; Kody
was too good a friend who didn't demand an excuse and
Jordyn found him to be a bothersome third wheel.

Jordyn shot a frustrated look to Kody, borrowing
against the future outrage derived from what was sure
to be Michael interrupting them all night. "Are we
going to have to spend the entire night with him?" she
asked, simultaneously nagging and pleading. It was the
job of a high school girlfriend to sever the boyfriend
from his friends, primarily his hopelessly single ones.
Jordyn had tried to do it cleanly, swiftly, with a
machete, but found the progress slow, like cracking an
exposed pipe and waiting for it to rust out. Michael
and her boyfriend were too much in high-school-boy-love
with each other. They assuaged each other's latent
insecurities too well for a clean divorce.

Kody punted. "I'll talk to him," he said
unconvincingly. Jordyn frowned.

Michael, meanwhile, considered himself as he crossed
the room to approach Emmaleigh. Just as Michael had
hoped, she was separated from her date, who was nowhere
to be seen. Emmaleigh stood in a small circle of
friends, all chatting, a small smile protesting
enthusiasm on her face.

In his own mind, Michael looked like the heroic boy
who crosses a crowded room in slow-motion during a
music video. To anyone else, he just sort of looked
like a guy who absent-mindedly leaves a room,
forgetting why he had entered it in the first place.

Michael fell in love with Emmaleigh more every time
he saw her, but tonight she was more stunning than he
had ever seen her. She wore a dress that may have been
commissioned just for her in a manner that would have
reaffirmed the designer's decision to go into fashion
were she to see her in it. And though it was
predictably conservative, there was something about it
that made it so much more alluring than the midriff-
exposing, semi-backless outfit that Reghan Weaver had
managed to wear past all four chaperones. There was a
class to it that became her. She defined the word
"elegant"; it had been inserted into the language
solely to describe her in this particular moment in
time. Every other recorded use of the word was merely
prologue. Every future use would be inadequate, its
definition forever altered to an unattainable standard.

Her brown hair spiraled into long curls over her
bare shoulders. This was atypical of the way she
usually wore it. It looked soft and pliable. Was that a

word that one could use to describe hair? He wasn't
sure and would err on caution by never using the word
in a sonnet for her were he ever afforded the chance.
He wanted so badly to run his hands through it, but
chided himself immediately for thinking something so
unspeakably lame and so distant from him that to even
articulate it in his thoughts gave him a burning shame.

With that, however, as if he had compelled it
telepathically, Emmaleigh ran her left hand through her
hair and over her ear, tucking back loose locks of
bouncing hair. Michael might have otherwise spent a
moment wondering too hard whether this was some kind of
sign from the universe or a deity or something else
equally unlikely. Instead, however, he caught the
glimmer of a little blue gem on a band on her ring
finger. It slowed him in his approach.

This was new since yesterday. Emmaleigh had
sometimes worn rings, but they were understated
sterling silver pieces. This was ostentatious and
showy. It was also a masculine ring, gaudy like a mood
ring or even a class ring, which no one seemed to wear
anymore. They had gone out of style as the graduating
classes became increasingly more college-bound and
subsequently less likely to hold onto accolades that
were merely stepping stones to greater erudition and
louder, hopefully sexier & more libertine curfew-less
binges. The last time he saw one worn was when a
wrestler won the state tournament in some disturbingly
low weight class and had the accolade etched into the
band, advertising his victory through every available
channel, from the discreet to the boorishly tacky.

What could it mean? he wondered. And which of the
eight digits advertised implications of one's romantic
status? Was it the right hand or left hand that
indicated exclusivity? And if so, to whom did it
belong? What were the circumstances in which it had
been given?

As he fixated on the ring and its potential
catastrophic meanings, Cayden returned from wherever he
had been, touching her on the small of the back to
indicate his return. She responded to the touch in a
manner that suggested it did not make her uncomfortable
and turned toward him, not reciprocating his touch but
smiling nevertheless.

This complicated things. His original plan had been
to say "Hi Emmaleigh" and then hope for a hostile alien
invasion, which would prompt Emmaleigh and her friends
to rally behind him for leadership, and after which
they would bond over their ordeal. She would be drawn
to his natural poise and heroism. Now he suddenly saw
it playing out more plausibly: "Hi Emmaleigh" would be
followed by the blank stares of Emmaleigh, four of her
friends, and her masculine date.

So he decided to ditch.

He abruptly turned 120 degrees and disguised his
emergency landing as a trip to the boys' bathroom. It
was casual, executed well, as if it had been his
destination the entire time. As if he were David
Naughton making a television commercial for peeing.

Not that anybody there knew that ancient reference.

Well, maybe one person.

The boys' bathroom off of the commons wasn't the type of bathroom that had a heavy door with handles that accumulated colorful colonies of pestilence; rather, there was a long, snaking hallway that led to the warm bosom of a long row of clean, sterile urinals divided and protected by high-density polyethylene partitions.

It was large, deliberately designed that way since it was adjacent to the room that performed two consecutive periods of lunch service. The size of the suite was amplified, however, due to its current lack of occupancy: the room was empty except for Braden Christensen, Class President and All-Around Supercilious Dick. That the student body had fallen for his glad-handing and elected him to its top college-resume bullet annoyed Michael. Braden noticed him but

chose not to acknowledge Michael's presence, until he
remembered he had a grievance against him. "Dude," he
started. "McKenzie's pissed."

Michael demurred. One, she was always pissed about
something insignificant. Two, he already knew. He'd
already been dressed down by her just a few minutes
ago.

"You know you're not allowed to bring girls from
other schools without registering them with the Spirit
Committee," Braden continued, pleased to harangue him
but pretending it annoyed him.

"Yeah, I've already been told," said Michael,
determining it was easier to apologize for a crime he
didn't commit than to protest his innocence. Why his
illusory date needed to be registered with any
committee was beyond him anyway. What were they going
to do? Run a background check? Say no and set up a
perimeter of state police to prevent her entry?

Braden continued. "It doesn't matter if they used to
go here. They still have to get permission."

"Wait, what?" This part was new to Michael, a useful
clue for learning the identity of the date he didn't
have.

"She used to go here. You didn't know that?" Braden
asked.

"No, I didn't," said Michael. "But I don't even know
who she is. So who is it?"

Braden was confused. He was surprised enough that
Michael could score a date as attractive as the girl
McKenzie had claimed he had invited in the first place.

How could Michael forget he invited her? Or that she accepted?

"Are you guys cousins or something?" Braden asked glibly.

"I don't think so," said Michael, growing tired of the exchange, but deciding to play along. "Why? Do you think that makes it grosser or sexier for when we boff later?"

Braden looked back at him, unsure of whether the question was a sincere one.

"I think sexier," said Michael.

Insincere, Braden concluded. He threw his paper towel in the trash and made for the exit, but not before throwing a parting barb.

"By the way," he said, "Nice catch last night."

"Yup, it was pretty clutch," Michael concurred.

Braden departed the bathroom with a grunt and left Michael alone. Michael looked at himself in the mirror with equal parts sympathy and contempt, nagged by a disquieting intrigue stemming from the twice-arisen rumor of a phantom date tracking him through the school. Perhaps a long lost middle school love returning to confess that she had never been able to get over him since leaving Crescent Lake? No, that couldn't possibly be it. As if he was worthy of being pined over. Besides, he'd have to tell her sorry, that he was already in love with someone else. Someone else who was on a date tonight with a different someone else.

Hmmm. Even hypothetically, this evening was not going as planned.

He fussed his fingers through his hair, attempting to improve it but only mussing it further. Sighing, he marched to the end of the empty line of urinals and unzipped himself.

It was at this moment that one of his dates entered, encroaching on his solitude.

"Michael?" she asked.

He didn't immediately turn, thinking he had hallucinated the voice. This was the boys' bathroom, after all. The little stick figure on the blue bathroom sign, ostensibly male by virtue of not wearing a dress and corroborated by what Michael assumed was the Braille word for "Men", was surely a force field that repelled the opposite gender from entrance. But he turned nevertheless.

It was her. The cheerleader who had sabotaged his game-winning catch. The cheerleader who had sabotaged his chance to impress Emmaleigh. The cheerleader whose sweater was a size too tight and skirt was an inch too high.

But her dress fit perfectly.

"There you are," she said. "I've been looking all over for you."

"You've been looking all over for me?" he replied incredulously. He was a master of witty repartee.

"I'm Lucy." She offered her hand, but Michael was preoccupied, his hands bound in the attempted act of urinating.

"Um, do you mind if I...?"

"Oh, sure," replied Lucy. She stood there, patiently, a polite smile on her face.

The large divider between each urinal didn't help
Michael to feel any more shielded from the singular
awkwardness of trying to pee while a beautiful, buxom
stranger waited on him. He tried and tried to fire a
spark that would ignite a stream of pee but was unable.
It didn't come. He remembered a particular track meet
that was held the previous spring at a disturbingly
unsavory facility. The mirrors were made of stainless
steel rather than glass and the toilet stalls of the
locker room were deprived of doors. The thought of a
situation that demanded their use horrified him. He had
literally dreamed about them during the occasional
night of tossing duress.

That feeling of exposure resonated with him now. He
tried to close his eyes and imagine that he were all
alone, but it didn't work. Nothing came. The engine
would not turn. He quietly re-zipped himself, hoping
she wouldn't notice that he had stood there for the
better part of a minute, failing and eventually
pretending to pee.

"Sorry about that," he apologized for some reason,
as if their roles had been reversed. He sheepishly
approached the faucet and rinsed his hands under the
water. She watched him do so with interest.

She offered again to shake his hand before he could
even dry it. "Lucy," she reiterated.

"Sure," he said, "My name is, uh..." It escaped him
somehow.

"I know who you are, Michael," she said. He
swallowed hard, surprised that she knew details about
him that even he didn't know, primarily his own first

name. He became aware of her warm, soft hand against his clammy, wet, sad hand.

"So do you have a date tonight?" she asked with unreserved optimism.

"No...?" Sometimes Michael uttered declarative sentences that had question marks at the end.

"Huh," she replied, the otherwise uninspired syllable spoken thoughtfully and pointedly, as if she had never been more intrigued at the mysteries of the universe. She produced and pinned a boutonnière on him, a red dicot that Michael couldn't identify. The colors & hues matched her dress. It paired them.

He looked at her blankly.

"So are you going to ask me to dance or what?" she aspired.

Key Change

Emmaleigh was slow-dancing with Cayden during the first ballad of the night when she became the second person in the entire fieldhouse to notice Michael across the dance floor with a surprisingly pretty girl in his arms.

"Who's that?" she asked Cayden, gesturing toward the couple. The girl was unrecognizable. There was no way she went to school here. Additionally, she knew that as recently as yesterday afternoon that Michael was dateless for Homecoming. What changed?

"I don't know," Cayden said, giving the strange girl a cursory look. "Why, are you jealous?" he asked, semi-teasingly. She laughed in reply to indicate to her date that she wasn't. Still, when the cadence of the dance permitted her a view, she took a second look and tried to make sense of the situation. Michael was trying to make sense of it too.

"So, uh, how do you know who I am?" Michael asked his date. She had led him to the dance floor where they caught one of the first slow dances of the evening. She was quick to abandon the safe, modest orbiting distance between the two that was so common on a high school dance floor, instead pressed closely against him, as if the night would quickly freeze and they had to conserve warmth. Though he was the boy, charged with doing the leading, it was Lucy who was giving directions.

She looked over both shoulders, as if checking for a tail, then whispered "I can't tell you."

Michael balked. This was just too weird in addition to too improbable. He looked into this mysterious person, trying to figure her out. She was attractive from sixty yards away; from within a foot she was stunning. Her interest in him made no sense.

She laughed. "Just kidding! Your name was listed in all the game programs. 'Michael Williams, number seven, five eleven, one-fifty-two, wide receiver/safety.' I saw you from the sideline and said 'I have to have him.'"

"Oh. Well just so you know, those numbers in the program are usually a little inflated."

"Is that right?" she asked, intrigued by otherwise banal information that was inelegantly substituted for conversation. "Well my numbers are thirty-four, twenty-four, thirty-three. And they're not inflated."

A moment passed as Michael wrapped his head around this information.

"I hope you don't mind that I invited myself to your dance."

"I hardly felt invited myself," he admitted.

She smiled. "Aren't we a pair of outlaws," she said, pressing herself against him, aggressively challenging the limits of the Pauli Exclusion Principle.

"What kind of car did you drive?"

Michael was embarrassed to tell her he didn't. "I walked."

"Oh. I bet you have strong legs," she rebutted.

Michael didn't know what that meant. The singer on the track broke into a second verse that repeated the chord progression of the first.

"This is a really nice school," she mused.

"Mmmm," was all Michael could muster with her body pressed so tight against him.

"This is a really nice gym," she added.

He groped at conversation. "They just built it," he replied. He knew she wasn't interested in the building but didn't know what else to say.

"I bet it has a really nice locker room," she continued. Michael didn't know what this meant. A few seconds went by before Michael walked into it.

"What?" he asked densely.

Though the music continued, she abruptly stopped their circling, freezing them together in a close, static pose. The other couples on the dance floor continued their slow swaying. Lucy, though, merely pressed further into her partner. "I've never really been one for dancing around," she said smoothly. She was speaking two languages at once.

Michael couldn't interpret either of them.

She leaned in and whispered into his ear. "What do you think? Want to take me to the locker room and give me a physical?"

Michael was nearly turned into a pillar of salt. He held his breath, expelling slowly, sounding like a punctured air mattress that was inopportunely spilling its ballast just as soon as it became necessary for its primary function.

"Ummmmmmm," he said, testing the utility of the word, if it could even be called that.

Lucy didn't mind the hesitation. It meant "yes"; the unambiguous affirmative response was lagging only a few seconds behind. She patiently waited, still locked so close to him that if any of the chaperones had witnessed their proximity, they'd surely be chased off the dance floor. But there was no danger of that; all four chaperones were conspicuously absent.

Michael didn't notice and didn't care. He was preoccupied by a realization borne of crisis, forced to confront the profound nature of his feelings for Emmaleigh. It must have been love, he thought, because every other girl he ever encountered may as well have been named Not Emmaleigh, and every other girl's features were only remarkable in that they were not Emmaleigh's. Lucy, this otherwise gorgeous, shapely girl whose smile was probably insured against loss or damage and for unlimited bodily harm against those hearts it would break, was among them. She was objectively, by any remotely conventional standard, attractive. 99th percentile. But to him, she was neither beautiful nor ugly nor gorgeous nor plain nor unprepossessing; she was simply Not Emmaleigh.

But Emmaleigh was on the other side of the fieldhouse-turned-ballroom, slow dancing with the second-best smile on the hardwood court. Even if he honorably carried a torch for her, it wasn't made any less heavy or burdensome by its charming futility. He considered this and weighed it against the not-so-subtle feeling that his hopeless pining for her had become a treadmill, a purgatory that prevented him from advancing through rites that others were rapidly accomplishing. Kody and Jordyn had already gone all the way. And scanning the dance floor, it appeared that Aiden Miller & Cloee Warren and Chayse Martin & Elliette Cooper were about to cross that Rubicon as well.

A key change in the slow-tempo alternative rock ballad happened to coincide with Michael's decision to foreclose on his tragically fruitless three-year pursuit and explore what was instead presented to him tonight.

"Can you wait here for a minute?" he asked Lucy. This was the affirmative response she was waiting for.

She smiled and held him a moment too long. "Hurry back," she said before biting her lip with such proficient subtlety that Michael saw it but didn't realize he saw it.

Michael cut from one side of the dance floor to the other. The chorus wasn't even over when Michael interrupted Kody & Jordyn's cozy slow-dance posture, shoving Jordyn away from his friend and confidant.

"Cutting in! " he announced. Jordyn protested but Michael had already absconded to the perimeter of the dance floor with her boyfriend where the few remaining wallflowers were taking refuge.

"I need some help," he said.

Kody was annoyed. "Obviously."

"Yesterday you told me you wanted to help me score, right?"

Kody shrugged. "Yeah, I guess."

There was a pause.

"So... Go," Michael said.

"What do you mean?" asked Kody.

Michael quickly grew frustrated. He wasn't good at
asking for help, especially at this. "Aren't you the
guy who's always droning on and on at football practice
about the one time you and Jordyn had sex at her
parents' lake cottage while they were at Blockbuster,
as if any of us gave a shit?"

Kody angrily hushed him. Peers were nearby and
eavesdropping. Michael sighed and lowered his voice.
"Well now I actually do, Ron Jeremy! So help me out!"

"Michael..."

"I mean, this is an area where compulsory state-
mandated education has really failed us, you know?"

Kody shook his head. "You weren't paying attention
in Mrs. Fuchs' class, were you?"

Michael wasn't paying attention now, either. He fell
into a diatribe. "They cram all this useless garbage
about Pythagoras and Euclid down our throats but never
teach us anything remotely useful, like taking off a
bra or giving a back massage or the Argentine tango--"

"Michael..."

"--highball cocktails--"

"Michael..."

"--tantric intercourse--"

"Michael!"

Michael caught himself, but not before adding one
more subject to the Revised Liberal Arts.

"...Falconry."

Kody looked over his shoulders to make sure no one
was eavesdropping. "Dude, I've got to tell you
something," he said, averting his eyes in shameful

confession. "Jordyn and I haven't gone all the way yet.
I exaggerated a little when I said that we had."

"Exaggerated?" Michael said curtly. He felt
betrayed. This was not the last time tonight he would
have that feeling. "You told me -- and I quote -- that
you two boned and it was hotter than two-a-days."

"I know I said that, but we didn't bone and it
wasn't hot. It was actually kind of embarrassing."

"She didn't want to?"

"No, she wanted to. She really wanted to." He paused
in embarrassment. "But I couldn't."

Michael didn't get it. "What do you mean?"

"I mean I couldn't. I was too nervous and I
couldn't, you know... I literally couldn't." He raised
a single finger in the air as a visual euphemism.
Michael was perplexed.

"Then why did you--?"

Kody anticipated the question. "I just wanted you to
catch up to the same page as me so we could...," he
paused, blushing, "I don't know? Share notes?"

Michael considered this surprising information. "You
haven't tried it since?" he inquired.

"We haven't had a chance. Her brother and his
friends are always around her house and my mom works at
home. Besides, I haven't even brought it up to her. It
was pretty embarrassing."

Michael struck a sentimental chord with his friend.
"Kody, do you remember that field trip we took to the
zoo in the fifth grade?"

Kody nodded, shrugged. "Yeah."

"Remember what those capuchin monkeys were doing?"

Kody stifled a laugh. It was an amusing memory that many parents had had recounted to them in vivid detail at their kitchen tables that night. "Yeah."

Michael's sentimentalism turned vicious. "Lower order primates with weird butts can do it and you can't."

Kody became defensive at the slight. "Listen, if it's so easy then why are you asking for my advice?"

Michael grunted and then muttered under his breath. "Amicus certus in re incerta cernitur."

"What?"

"Lucy wants to... you know..."

"Lucy?" Kody had no idea who this person was.

"Remember that cheerleader from the game? She's here. That's her name. And I guess she's totally into me." Michael indicated her across the room. Kody followed his gesture and, sure enough, there was the treacherous cheerleader, looking absolutely striking. The only girl in the building with opera gloves. She looked like a liner photo in a Blink 182 album, a one-thousand-page dissertation by Pierre Bezier.

Kody was nevertheless repulsed. "Dude, don't do it."

"Just yesterday you told me I needed to score!" Michael rebutted.

"Yeah, with Reghan Weaver maybe, but never with girls from other schools. Let me tell you a universal truth about life, Mike. The only reason a girl like that would date some guy from another school -- a/k/a you -- would be if all the guys at her school already knew that she had every form of hepatitis, even Hep-C."

Michael fumed and stammered, averting his eyes to avoid Kody's ugly point. Its validity was inconvenient.

"Or maybe some other exotic disease," Kody continued. "Did you know that syphilis, if untreated, is fatal?"

Michael didn't reply. He was suddenly distracted by Abigayle Albright and Jaden Phillips, who were kissing in a remarkably immodest way. This was unusual on its own, but was compounded by the fact that Abigayle was terminally shy, never speaking in class. That she would have her tongue in someone else's mouth in such a brazen manner, surrounded by peers, was surprising. Michael only partially heard Kody's mocking tirade against him.

"...But before syphilis kills you, it makes you go insane," Kody concluded. There was a pause. Kody had a sudden break-through realization: "Maybe you already have syphilis!" he said. This would explain a lot about his friend.

Jaden's hand breached the territory over Abigayle's posterior and gently groped. Surely this was a violation of the student code of conduct, Michael thought.

Kody smacked him twice on the face in an annoyed, maternal manner. "Are you even listening to me?"

Michael flinched. "Something about syphilis?" he said in the same manner as when he got caught daydreaming in class.

Kody stared at him for a moment, sizing something up. Michael didn't know what the look meant and self-consciously probed his own face, wondering whether he had something embarrassing stuck to him.

"What about Emmaleigh?" Kody asked pointedly, without blinking. He drew the phrase out.

Michael shrugged defensively. "What about Emmaleigh?" It was childish rhetoric, an attempt to conceal his patent aversion to taking a risk.

Kody looked at him as if he were transparent. Michael capitulated.

"It's just, she's here with somebody else. So maybe, you know, I ought to just get over her. And some super hot girl who for some reason wants to hook up with me seems like a good place to start."

"Are you listening to yourself?" Kody replied in a cold manner that, were this advice to come from anyone other than his best friend, would have been cruel and glib rather than reaffirming. "You haven't even attempted to be 'under her'. The truth is, Emmaleigh is here with someone else because nobody else, including you, asked her." He mocked him. "'Oh, Kody, there's this girl in my homeroom class. Oh my God! We were destined to be together. Wait, nevermind, she's on a date with the only other guy to ever ask her out so I guess I'll just go hang out with some unexplained mystery slut and contract a delightful venereal disease instead.'"

Michael looked away. This was cold water in the face.

"I'm not saying this to make you feel bad. I'm saying it because I'm your friend. Are you going to feel okay if you look back on this next summer and know

you didn't even take the chance? People don't regret
taking chances, you know. They regret missing them."
Kody removed his wristwatch, some analog piece with a
stainless steel band. "Here, I want you to borrow
this."

Michael accepted it. "Your watch? Why?"

"It's a reminder. Remember yesterday when you choked
and asked Emmaleigh what time it was?"

"Yeah," he said, displeased at the memory.

"Well, it's later than you think." Kody indicated
the center of the dance floor, where Cayden and
Emmaleigh were still dancing, even though the tempo had
picked up again.

"I've got to go find Jordyn," Kody said before
slipping back into the party. "Good luck, Mike."

And just like that, Michael was alone again. He
suffered chronostasis as he looked down at the watch,
then glanced back up to the dance floor where Emmaleigh
and her date remained. He schemed for a moment and even
took a step toward them, but then hesitated. He
realized he needed to take at least a few minutes to
engineer a plan that might rescue her, or at least
clear his head. He would take the chance, he resolved.
He had to. He wouldn't forgive himself not to. But he
had to judiciously plan his actions & words. He
wouldn't half-ass it like he did 20 minutes ago or
Friday afternoon or two weeks ago when he penned that
note or two semesters ago when he tried but
ignominiously failed to help her install the Quadratic
Formula on her TI-83 before finals or any of those

other sad, similar oblique attempts since freshman
year.

He stole to the end of the fieldhouse, the little
round lights of the suspended mirror ball futilely
scanning over him like underpowered searchlights. He
leaned gently against one of the solid double-door
exits and quietly slipped outside to contemplate his
grand romantic gesture.

Win Emmaleigh or Die Trying.

It was a surprisingly warm night, Michael noted, as he walked the perimeter of the school. He moved with urgency, calculating, scheming, groping for some semblance of a plan to steal away the girl of his dreams from the guy of every girl's. He looked down at the watch that Kody had clasped over his wrist. Michael had quit wearing some cheap Casio in the 9th grade after the battery died and had, since then, become unused to wearing a watch. Still, this one was particularly uncomfortable and wore like an albatross. The cold face looked back at him, offering him no suggestions, only on-the-second reminders that time was fleeting.

He slunk down to the sidewalk that ran adjacent to the parking lot and drew his hands through his hair. The distinguished part he had drawn in hours ago was

now wrecked beyond recognition and he began to look
more like himself. He closed his eyes and took
inventory of his few desirable assets.

In the quiet darkness and perfidious absence of his
own useful thoughts is where he heard it: the distinct
sounds of somebody doin' it. He opened his eyes and
glanced around the parking lot. He couldn't identify
where, but it was definitely happening. Somewhere
close.

He stood and surveyed the parking lot as the short
bursts of enthusiasm grew louder, the cadence
increasing, and followed them to the source. The
halogen lights over the parking lot provided enough
visibility to identify a tiny red sedan, its color and
its spartan form both reminiscent of the most romantic
20th-century fascist movements. Its manual-operated
windows were veiled in the foggy by-product of the
wanton abandonment of its occupants' self-restraint.
The parked vehicle bounced slightly in a surreal tempo
as if it were dancing under headphones. He could
roughly make out the silhouetted form of someone
sitting upright in the rear passenger seat. But
suddenly, abruptly, the moaning stopped. The gentle
rocking stopped. It was as if the car itself realized
that it was being spied on.

A moment went by in which Michael wondered whether
he had imagined the whole scene. He looked cautiously
at the car, the way an animal might look at a fake owl
posted over a home garden, and considered for a
fraction of a second whether the automobile had
achieved technological singularity and was making a

mark of him, like it was intentionally distracting him, as if conspiring velociraptors might quickly descend on him from his blindsides. He glanced uneasily over each shoulder.

But then, the back door cracked open, and, from the uncomfortable yet sufficient economy of the Plymouth Horizon, a girl stepped out, replacing her shoes and smoothing her dress back to its original form.

Michael ducked, suddenly aware of his own open-jawed profile, reluctant to be caught in the act of such egregious voyeurism.

He turned and scrambled behind a dumpster at the end of a short alley, re-entering the school building through the first door he saw available.

An Insatiable Desire to Fornicate

Gabriel the Janitor sat at his shop desk, poring over the previous year's yearbook. He was charged with discovering two people, a task he'd been working on since Labor Day three years earlier. One he had found last spring. The second was still a mystery. He flipped the pages, groping for clues.

That's when Michael entered, retreating from the parking lot of sin and hedonism.

The janitor sat up at Michael's awkward entrance, as if he had anticipated him, as if his appearance were pre-ordained. "There you are!" he exclaimed. This was the third time tonight Michael had heard that phrase spoken with such specific interest.

"Oh no."

"You've arrived, just as prophesied," said Gabriel to Michael, the irony alarmingly missing from his grave tone. Michael the prophet balked, turned around and looked behind him, trying to identify the person the janitor was addressing.

"You didn't have sex with anyone tonight, did you?" asked the janitor.

"Me?" asked Michael, confused.

"Yes, you!" scolded the janitor.

Michael scoffed. "Who are you, my mom?"

"Answer me!"

"No, janitor, I didn't have sex with anyone or anything ever. Are you satisfied? Are you pleased?"

Gabriel breathed a sigh of relief. "Good. You get laid tonight and the world is going to end."

Michael had heard plenty of scare tactics posing as reasons for abstinence since the 6th grade, but this was something new altogether.

"Did Kody put you up to this? Because I get it, okay? She's dirty. She's a whore. She's got alllll the hepatitis, even Hep-C!"

"It's worse than that, Michael," Gabriel said.

"Hep-D!" groused Michael. "Hep-E-F-G-H-I-J-K-LMNOP!"

Gabriel shook his head. "She's a demon. They all are."

"What?"

"And they're here to get you. To destroy you."

"Who are?"

"I just said. Any girl who comes on to you."

"What are you talking about?"

The janitor frowned. "You'd better sit down, Michael. This is going to be sobering." Michael looked around; there was nowhere to sit. He wouldn't have sat anyway.

"How do you know my name?" Michael asked. The janitor ignored him.

"Are you familiar with the Bible?"

"I guess," Michael reluctantly replied.

"Lucifer?" asked the janitor.

"He's the bad guy, right?"

The janitor nodded and informed him of something shocking: "He's an alumnus of Crescent Lake High School. And do you know what tonight is, Michael?"

Michael shrugged. What?

"IT'S HOMECOMING," the janitor said, grimly.

There was a pause while Michael measured the janitor's sanity.

"Listen," Michael started, noting the janitor's embroidered name tag. "Gabe. I'd love to stay and chat but my friends are probably waiting for me to not be stabbed by any late-shift heroin addicts tonight."

"Your friends don't care what you're doing," Gabriel curtly informed him.

"That's uncalled for," Michael replied, concealing the fact that it was probably at least partially true. But who was this strange janitor to be such a jerk?

"What I mean is that they're probably indulging their INSATIABLE DESIRE TO FORNICATE as we speak."

"Insatiable desire to fornicate...?"

Gabriel nodded with knowing sagacity. "The entire student body has turned totally horny, their inhibitions dissolved, per biblical prophesy."

Michael stared at him for a long time.

Gabriel nodded. "Anyone who entertains the notion of intercourse tonight is going to have it. But it gets worse."

"Okay," Michael said, cautiously playing along.

"Every student who has sex tonight is going to conceive a demon. Unless Lucifer is stopped, those demons will gestate and be birthed at dawn. Soldiers in Lucifer's army of the rapture. You know what this means, right?"

"Yeah," said Michael. "It means you lost your medicine."

Gabriel slowly shook his head.

"A sun of sackcloth. Rivers of blood. The final battle between good and evil, the dragon and the lamb. Armageddon. And you, Michael, are the only one who can stop it."

There was a long pause.

"Maybe they just rolled onto the floor or something?" Michael asked, looking underneath the table for the janitor's absent prescriptions.

"Michael!" Gabriel interjected. "This is serious. This is--"

"Look, as flattered as I am that you want me to take part in your holy janitor apocalypse--"

"I'm not a janitor. I'm an angel," replied Gabriel. "From Heaven," he added hastily to avoid confusion.

Michael sniffed the air for evidence of hallucinogenics. The results were inconclusive.

"I'm sensing skepticism," said Gabriel.

Michael did not dignify the statement with a response. But Gabriel could prove it.

"Michael, do you speak Latin?"

"No," said Michael, unimpressed.

"Never studied it?"

"No," he reprised.

"Not once?"

"No, I said!"

"Es certus?" asked Gabriel.

"Yes, I'm sure!" Michael exclaimed, losing patience. Gabriel smiled. Yes, Michael was the one. He returned to the yearbook he had been studying prior to Michael's fortuitous entrance. "I have something to show you. Come here and take a look at this. It's important."

Gabriel crossed the room to show Michael some compelling piece of evidence, some old dusty yearbook, briefly turning his back to him. Gabriel flipped through the pages, identified a particularly damning black & white photo, and turned dramatically back to Michael.

"How do you explain this!" he said.

But Michael was gone. He had stolen the opportunity to escape, slipping out the door quietly thanks to his accidental soft soles.

"Damn it," cursed the angel janitor.

Eyeliner Calligraphy

Kody had gone to use the bathroom and, when he returned, found that his girlfriend had mysteriously disappeared. All that remained in her place was a note with his name written in her handwriting, the calligraphy inked with an eyeliner pencil. Kody glanced around the arena, trying to see whether Jordyn was hiding somewhere around him, playing an odd prank. Unable to find her, he unfolded the note. "Costume Shop" were the only two words written within, a distinct Lewis Carroll intrigue to it.

He looked again around the room but couldn't find her. Putting his jacket back on, he exited the fieldhouse, enlisted into a scavenger hunt of sorts.

Michael had slipped out of the custodial shop but didn't make it very far down the hallway that led to the commons, which itself led to the fieldhouse, where he could rendezvous with the remainder of the student body, which was rumored to be cursed and fornicating. Yeah right.

"There you are!" exclaimed Lucy.

"Ugh," Michael said to himself. He had never been so popular. It was a queer feeling.

"I've been looking all over for you!" she continued. "I thought we were going to... you know..." She bit her lip and shoved her hips into him.

"Dance?" inquired Michael.

"Go someplace quiet and give me paraplegia."

Michael laughed uncomfortably, the same way he did back in the 7th grade when they pushed play on the documentary videotape and a staid, baritoned voice-over man said "sexual intercourse" with a tone and authoritative enthusiasm that matched the animatronics at the Disney Hall of Presidents.

"Lucy?" he asked her cautiously.

"Yes, sexy?" she said. Her hand had already found its way into his hair. She made gentle circles in it with her index finger.

"Are you a demon sent from Hell to destroy me?"

She hesitated, looking at him with precisely the kind of look such a question would elicit.

"Ha! Just kidding. But seriously, do you have hepatitis or any other communicable diseases?" he inquired.

She raised an eyebrow. "You don't talk to a lot of girls, do you?"

Michael was suddenly reminded of the time he pulled away from a Wendy's drive-through window without ordering after being intimidated by the sultry female voice on the intercom. No doubt she was gorgeous. No doubt he was an intrusion in her life. What could he offer her that someone else couldn't?

"No," he shook his head. "Not really."

"Let me make this easy for you," said Lucy. "I'm not dirty, and I'm not easy, either. In fact," she said, biting her lip, "I've been saving myself for you." Her arms snaked their way around his shoulders and she pulled herself against him. He had never been so aware of the pressure of breasts pressed against his body.

"That's..." he wanted to say "flattering," but instead replied, "...kind of weird."

She smiled at him seductively and ran her hand again through his hair, as Michael racked his brain trying to calculate the probability of this happening outside of the plot of a late-night Cinemax movie, the kind he had seen through grainy clarity on his parents' basement television when he plugged the coaxial cable directly into the set.

Although it didn't really make any sense, the explanation that Lucy was indeed some supernatural being who sought to destroy him as part of some nefarious plot to enslave mankind was, sadly, the most probable explanation. He decided to terminate the relationship in its infancy, before it could get too serious. This was his most practiced move when it came to the fairer sex.

"So what do you think? Do you want to?" she asked, pressing further into him.

"You know, I just don't think this is going to work out. I'm an Aries, and you're a... whatever you are. I just don't think there's anything long term here."

"Oh I'm sure there's something long here." She groped her way along the fabric of his pants. "Oh, yes. Very long."

He grimaced. "You'll meet someone new."

"I think I'm meeting someone new right now," she rebutted, her soft hand confidently planted where none other had yet ventured.

Resisting was futile, he determined. He girded himself, improvising a new escape plan. "Okay, fine. Let's do this," he said, resolutely. "Let's do the sex now."

"Yeah?" said Lucy, "You want it?"

"Yes. We are going to have sexual intercourse. I am going to..." he paused, trying to summon something sexy. It was as if, after faking his way through two years of Spanish classes, he had without warning been parachuted into Spain and had to find his way home among a foreign population. His words were awkward and clumsy and his diction was slightly off and his sentences took too long to form. "I am going to slam that vagina." Then he growled for some reason.

Lucy, instead of being repulsed, smiled and licked her upper lip, another indication that there was something about this tryst that was fundamentally contrived & unholy. She reached for his belt, the convenient reversible kind with black leather on one side and brown on the other, and started to unbuckle him.

"Wait!" said Michael. He gestured to a faculty restroom about 30 feet down the hall. "I read that you last longer if you rub one out first. Let me go crank one out and then we'll... you know, do it for, uh..." Michael wasn't sure how long sex lasted. "We'll do it for a long time relative to the typical duration, with which I'm very familiar. Because I've had lots of sex."

Lucy smiled. Michael didn't know that she knew the statement, with divine certainty, to be false.

"No. Right now," she said, calling his bluff. "I want it right now."

"But what if it's over too fast?" asked Michael rhetorically, thinking he had persuaded her of the value of his postponement.

"Then we'll go twice."

"Oh," he replied. "Good thinking." Lucy, with little
warning, suddenly ripped the belt from the loops of his
pants as if starting a lawn mower. As she went for his
fly, Michael suddenly "remembered" something.

"Oh yeah, I forgot!" He raised an eyebrow and tried
to say it as seductively as possible. "I also need to
take my insulin." She hesitated, released him and
stared at him in an are-you-kidding-me kind of way. "I
also need to drop a deuce," he said as he slipped
toward the door. "And charge up a videocamera." She
narrowed her eyes, trying to figure him out.

"I'm going to record it.

"That way I can watch it later.

"The intercourse," he clarified. "Not my insulin
shot.

"That wouldn't be very sexy," he said, and then
retreated through the bathroom door and turned the
deadbolt lock behind him.

Lucy waited patiently for several minutes but
finally tired and approached the door. She knocked
first but received no answer. So she tried the handle.
Michael had locked it behind him, but Lucy was able to
effortlessly breach it somehow.

She swung open the door to a vacant 90 square feet
of men's faculty restroom. Stepping through the bright
fluorescent light of the lavatory, she approached the
toilet stall and slowly opened the door to reveal that
it was uninhabited. Above the toilet was a displaced
drop-ceiling tile. Michael had climbed the toilet and

escaped through the ceiling, shuffling across a series of steel joists en route to the rest of his ordeal.

Lucy sighed. She wanted to be the one who got him. But it might be as difficult as it was prophesied to be.

Kody entered the costume shop that used to be the
old band room. If the lights were on, one could still
see the dozens of plaques from state band festivals
that adorned the high, sound-proofed walls, claimed in
triumph years earlier by students who had put hundreds
of hours of study and practice into their craft, raised
them as laurels of their accomplishment, and left them
suspended there uncelebrated, practically abandoned, in
the subsequent years since accepting their diplomas and
becoming whatever they were to become. No one had even
taken them down and moved them into the new, more
spacious band room when the school added a new
performing arts wing. The school simply earned new ones
that would prove how lauded the band students were,
plaques that were, once again, left behind by their

champions like ticker tape that no one had decided to clean up. Proof of both the victories and the ephemeral thrill of those victories.

The room, now transformed into a glorified closet, hosted racks upon racks of wardrobe and props for stage plays, period dress for Our Town & Grease & Bye Bye Birdie & all those other productions that would debut immortal stage legends every semester. Kody moved through the racks. He had been instructed to meet Jordyn here, but he still wasn't sure why. He called her name while trolling through the aisles of wardrobe in a somewhat hesitant manner, as if he was unsure whether she was even there. As if he expected someone else -- or something else -- to answer his salutation.

"Jordyn...?

"Jordyn...?

"Jordyn, are you here...?"

He reached the end of the third aisle but still received no response. It was dark. The only light in the room was that from the parking lot streetlights that managed its way though the two far windows. His eyes were adjusting, though. He could tell that the sewing mannequins were merely that, nothing worse. Nothing more sinister.

He turned the fourth row. "Jordyn?"

That's when he heard something.

"Stop right there, soldier."

Kody turned 180 degrees to find the silhouette of his girlfriend there. She seemed to be holding a prop rifle. It was trained on him. "Hands up," she demanded.

Kody did as he was told, smiling cautiously. "What
are you doing?"

"I told you," she said, advancing on him, "I wanted
to get away from the party for a little while."

"If you're trying to hide from Mike, it's okay. I
talked to him. He promised to spend the rest of the
night annoying Emmaleigh. Or pouting." He scratched his
head. "I'm not sure which. The point is, we're alone."

Kody himself didn't even realize the gravity of
their being alone. As Jordyn advanced into the light
encroaching through the window, Kody could see that she
was freed from her evening dress. Her prop rifle, a
relic from some performance of South Pacific, was
complemented by a matching prop helmet of a WWII
leatherneck. The rest of her scant attire was comprised
of various burlesque items collected from the costume
shelves and her own frilly underwear, which had been
carefully selected earlier that evening because she
knew that they were to be revealed.

"That's not totally why I told you to meet me here,"
she said, halting within whispering distance from him.

"Oh," said Kody, a bit densely.

She dropped the rifle and swung around his neck a
feather boa, something from a spirited performance of
La Cage au Folles that had been inelegantly selected
and subsequently angered some of the parents and sent
the sponsor of the spring musical into involuntary
retirement.

"Oh!" he said, realizing it.

"Just relax," said Jordyn as she removed his jacket.
"It'll be ok."

Only seven semesters ago, that same room had hosted
the practice of the spring musical orchestra. One of
their festival plaques hung on the wall above them.
They had performed the score to polite accolades.

Come to me, here I am, come to me
Bali Ha'i

Kody and Jordyn were not remotely the first teenage
couple to copulate in that room.

No one noticed as Michael was birthed into the hallway from the drop-ceiling above. They were too involved with each other. Indeed, Michael was even too involved with himself. He had Emmaleigh so much on his mind that he didn't notice two sophomores in the shallow entryway to one of the geometry classrooms, plunging into the irrecoverable depths of physical intimacy.

Moments later he had smoothly re-inserted himself in the sparkling fieldhouse. When he arrived he was no worse off from Lucy's wanton assault save for some dust and shards of mineral fiber that stuck to his suit like glitter. He climbed the stairs that led to the mezzanine over the gym, mostly comprised of a four-lane indoor track that ran the perimeter of the gymnasium, designed for those first weeks of spring when the snow had not yet left the outdoor fields. From this vantage, he could survey the entire gymnasium. Before he could begin his surveillance, however, he was greeted by a classmate named Madalyn.

"Hey, Mike," she said to him. "Lookin' good."

Michael looked himself over, the wrong shoes on his feet and his belt missing, which affected the structural integrity of his poorly creased pants. His hair and jacket were covered in dust. There was something obviously unkempt about himself; even he was unimpressed with his own appearance. He concluded that she was being sarcastic but decided to let it go.

"Hey, Madalyn," he replied. "Have you seen Emmaleigh around?"

"Nope. It's just us. Want to go someplace and be alone? Maybe talk? Maybe..." She batted her eyes.

Michael paused.

"What?"

She dismissed him as a lost cause and moved on. Michael didn't care. He returned his attention to the gymnasium dance floor, scanning for Emmaleigh, his saber drawn, ready to tilt at windmills. Only a moment passed before he was interrupted again.

"Hey man, have you seen Madalyn Moran come through here?" asked a boy named Caemron who was known to be kind of sleazy, a student custodian of A/V equipment who had once accidentally left a mini-DV tape in one of the school cameras with footage that he had surreptitiously shot in a Mervyn's fitting room. He was given a mere in-school suspension because his parents were somehow connected to the school board. He should have been prosecuted.

"Yeah, just a second ago. Why? What's going on?"

"I don't know, man. Someone must have spiked the punch 'cause everyone's turned totally horny."

The words echoed in his head: Everyone's turned totally horny?

"What did you just say?"

"It's like a John Hughes porno in here! Everybody's hooking up!"

Michael considered this and looked across the festively decorated court for a second time. There really didn't seem to be anything remarkable going on down there. Students dancing, socializing. Then he noticed Spenser Schmitt making out unapologetically with Maddison Kelly. Their disparate levels of both beauty and social rank, not to mention their indiscreet level of decorum, made it a peculiar pairing. He shrugged it off and tried to find Emmaleigh again.

Caemron interrupted his surveillance. "Looks like I picked a good night to go stag," he said. "It's like an all you can eat taco buffet, you know what I'm saying?"

"No," said Michael judgmentally. He didn't know what the expression meant, but he was sure it was untoward.

"Fish tacos!" clarified Caemron. Michael still didn't get it. Caemron didn't wait to offer an explanation; he was off to claim a line in the buffet. Michael dismissed it, refocusing his efforts on finding Emmaleigh. But as he scanned the gymnasium he was interrupted again.

"There you are!" said a female voice.

"Jesus Christ, again?" Michael said aloud, turning to the latest person to seek him out. It was Jessica

Henry, who had once attended Crescent Lake but had
moved away in the sixth grade. She was always pretty,
but now she was older, prettier, curvier. Michael
hardly recognized her. Was this the phantom date that
Braden had been talking about?

"Jess? Is that you?" he asked.

"I have to talk to you," she said.

"About what?"

"Something's going on," she replied. "Something
significant. Something ancient."

Michael looked down at the gymnasium floor. Spenser
& Maddison had mysteriously disappeared, swept away
somewhere by a pernicious undertow.

"What's going on?" asked Michael.

"I can tell you, but not here. Someplace quiet.
Someplace where they can't find us."

Michael looked over both shoulders, confused at the
pronoun "they" and the reason they should be in danger,
and then looked back at her with the same skepticism.
Nevertheless he acceded. She led him away from the
party, from the fieldhouse, and into the library, deep
into the stacks.

"It should be safe here," she said after reaching a
sufficiently solitary place of refuge, upon which they
shared a silent, seemingly tacit moment. Michael
shrugged, imploring her to reveal whatever it was she
knew about whatever it was that was going on that
seemed apparent to her & Caemron & the weird janitor
but had completely eluded him.

"So what's this ancient, significant something?" he pressed.

She paused. It was a long, ominous, disquieting pause. He didn't know that he was in the eye of the coming storm. Her eyes darted over and past his shoulders, reconnoitering the room to make sure it was safe before proceeding.

"I have to have you," she finally said.

"Huh?"

She grabbed him violently, pressing herself against him. "Please, Michael, you have no idea how bad I've wanted this, how long I've wanted you."

She had AN INSATIABLE DESIRE TO FORNICATE. Gabe the janitor was right. Michael attempted to push her away. She brought her lips to his neck and kissed him in an immodest way that was reserved for other girls and less insecure guys.

"Please! I want you so bad! We have to be together! I've thought about you every day since my family moved away!"

"Oh shit. Oh shit," repeated Michael to himself.

"You've been on my mind for so long. I came tonight just to see you! In the hope that I could just see you and get the chance to talk to you again, to look into those brown eyes as you sink yourself inside me."

Michael fumbled and tripped over both himself and her terrifying licentiousness, trying to extricate himself. "Let's just be friends," he demurred uneasily.

"We'll be friends," she said with a timbre reserved for moments like this, "Friends who can't go swimming tomorrow!" She tugged at his tie and the knot slipped, exposing his collar. She kissed it violently. Michael struggled against it, scooting on his back away from her. She reached behind her back and unzipped her dress, exposing bare shoulders that were, heretofore, the most nude he had ever seen a female. This practically turned Michael into Rain Man.

"Let's just be friends! Let's just be friends!" He chanted the phrase as if it possessed some type of mystic sorcery.

"Shhhh," she said to him with the calming reassurance of a date rapist. She unclasped her bra and was exposed to him. He was accidentally exploring all kinds of new territory tonight. He continued to perseverate.

"Let's just be friends! Let's just be friends!"

"Shhhh..." she said again, raising a finger to his lips and seizing him over his pants.

That's when Michael, instinctively and without thinking, said the phrase in a language that he had never been formally taught:

"Sit iustum esse amicos! Sit iustum esse amicos!"

And just like that, as if by magic, Jessica disappeared, exploding into a cloud of locusts, hundreds of them, veritably a cloud of them that could blacken the daytime sky.

"Jesus Christ! SICK!" exclaimed Michael, jumping and falling backward at the same time. "Sick sick sick sick sick sick!" He brushed several of the bugs off of him and bolted for the exit to the library.

Just before reaching the soft green glow of the mounted exit sign that hung above the entryway, a hypothesis occurred to Michael. He decided to test it. He turned back into the stacks until he reached the collection of old yearbooks that had accumulated throughout the otherwise uncelebrated history of Crescent Lake High School.

His finger ran across the shelf of ancient yearbooks and, at random, picked one that looked like it might be ancient. The 1978 Laker. He flipped through some pages.

And sure enough, there he was, listed among the senior class. "Lucifer." A handsome guy with dated hair and a very wide Windsor knot. "Best Smile. Captain, Track & Field."

Michael dropped the yearbook to the floor and reached for another at random.

He opened the 1996 Laker. There he was again:
Lucifer. The exact same guy as before. The same eyes.
The same smile. But different hair. Grunge-vogue. A
thinner tie with a looser knot, a more muted suit.
Voted Most Likely to Succeed.

He sent it to the floor with the 1978 edition,
hurling it away from him as if it were crawling with
wood roaches.

Picked up 1986. He was there too. The exact same
eyes and smile as before. Different hair. A tuxedo for
some reason. Senior Quote: "Kyrie eleison... Where I'm
going will you follow?"

Michael didn't know it, but he was being mocked with
80s pop lyrics in yearbooks that were printed before he
had even started kindergarten by a rival he didn't even
know he had. It was an elaborate level of insult.

He started to flee but hesitated and returned into
the stacks. In the reference section, he threw open the
heavy dictionary that sat like a religious tome on its
own podium. He flipped through the pages until he
reached his destination:

Insatiable (adj.) In'sey'sha'ble. 1.
Incapable of being sated. 2. Unable to reach a
level of satisfaction. 3. Unquenchable.

Michael turned ashen and jumped when he heard his
name spoken by a female voice. He turned to find Mrs.
Fuchs. He hadn't heard her enter. It was almost as if
she materialized there.

"Michael? Are you okay?"

He was still in shock from having witnessed the first girl to ever expose herself to him explode into a thick cloud of soulless orthoptera.

"Um..." was all he could manage to articulate.

"I think I can help you. I heard earlier that you were having trouble finding the clitoris." She looked at him a bit too solicitously. "Do you still need any help?"

Michael swallowed hard.

"I have a master's degree, you know."

Michael blinked.

"Have you seen Gabe the janitor?"

Cayden and Emmaleigh had found their way to the
courtyard outside of the school. It was an intimate
environment, designed with concrete and earthen rows of
an outdoor amphitheater and trees that flowered in
springtime. Though the dull bass of the DJ's subwoofers
and elements of student conversation wafted outside,
the two were otherwise alone. And though it was after
dark in late September, it was still warm. All in all
it was a very pleasant environment. There was a
comfortable, contented pause as they both lay in the
soft grass under the stars. Cayden broke it.

"What do you want, Mary?"

Emmaleigh turned to him. "What?"

"You want the moon?"

She was confused. "What are you talking about?"

He tried his best Jimmy Stewart, which was surprisingly good. "'Cause if you want it, I'll lasso it out of the sky and you can eat it and it'll be delicious and moon beams will shoot out of your face and we'll buffalo dance until V-J day!"

Emmaleigh laughed, getting the reference. "God, I love that movie!"

"Me too," Cayden replied. "I've actually cried at the end of it.

"Really?" asked Emmaleigh.

Cayden nodded, confessing his humility. "Like a little girl who just watched her pony get put down by a scary clown."

"That's not funny," Emmaleigh replied, feigning indignation. "I used to have a pony, and she WAS put down by a scary clown."

"I'm so sorry," Cayden said with too much stilted empathy, "Can I console you?"

"You can try," she said. It was banter but also an invitation.

He patted her on the shoulder, rigidly, with deliberate awkwardness. "There, there," he said in monotone. "Don't be sad about your tragically dead pony." She laughed.

There was a spark. They looked at each other in a way that few do. Perfect constellations hung in the night sky above them.

Emmaleigh studied them above. "Makes you feel small, doesn't it?"

"Actually, no," Cayden replied. He smiled. "When I'm
with you, I feel pretty..." he paused, searching for
the right word. "Significant." She smiled back.

He sat up. "Emmaleigh, where do you think you're
going to go to school next year?"

"I don't know yet. Probably close to home. I haven't
made up my mind."

"I haven't either," he said. "But I got this
incredible offer this week to play at U.C.L.A."

"That's unbelievable! Are you going to take it?"

"I'm not sure yet."

"You should! That would be such an amazing
opportunity."

He looked at her for a moment. "The problem is," he
started, "I'm sort of thinking about a different
opportunity I'm afraid I'd regret missing." There was a
moment. She looked down at the ring he had offered her
earlier in the evening. While she considered it, he
slid his hand over to hers. She accepted it.

They sat in contented silence. The stars continued
burning in perfect concert above.

    Michael was at a full sprint down the hallway,
heading toward the janitorial shop that was tucked into
the most inconvenient place in the school. Something
about exploding his former middle school classmate had
activated his fight-or-flight response. He flew.

    When he arrived, he found it empty. No Gabe. No
evidence of anyone, except for a copy of last year's
yearbook left open on a work bench. Michael flipped
through the warm pages, looking for clues that could
explain the janitor's earlier eerie premonition or
Jessica's horrifying transformation. In the 11th grade
photo section, someone had taken a red Sharpie marker
and had crossed out the faces of dozens of Michael's
female classmates in large obscene X's, adding
illegible notes in a foreign alphabet throughout the
margins. His own picture, a black & white embarrassment

made more embarrassing by the dumb smile on his face, was circled several times in green ink. The highlighting made the dumb smile appear even dumber. It also made this creepy situation a not-insignificant bit creepier.

His mind raced. He had to locate this person who had predicted some bizarre supernatural phenomenon that until five minutes ago sounded like the ravings of a lunatic. Maybe he could find a way to page him. A thought occurred to him, and he ransacked the shop until he found a set of building keys. Minutes later, he arrived at the main office, unlocking it with his janitorial skeleton key, and seized the public address microphone, flipping the red-lighted switch on the control panel.

In the fieldhouse, Michael's voice over the meager PA was inaudible underneath Brian McKnight's smooth baritone as it was broadcast over the DJ's enormous speakers. In the remainder of the building, however, his voice resonated among the dark, empty classrooms and vacant hallways like God's.

"Gabe the Janitor. Gabe the Janitor. It's Michael. You know, that one guy? I need you to meet me in the custodial shop. Again, meet me in the custodial shop."

The principal's office was only thirty feet away from that microphone, and Principal Strong sat up at the announcement.

"Who is that?" asked Señora Carroll, who was sharing his flask and his company and his dark office.

"Shhh," said the principal, hushing her. He waited a moment to determine whether the reprobate who had

somehow seized the microphone had bored of his crime
and wandered off. To confront the culprit would be, at
this moment, inconvenient. Satisfied that whoever had
commandeered the PA had left, Principal Strong returned
to the task at hand.

By the time Michael returned to the custodial shop,
Gabriel was already there. Michael partially expected
him to be there, but still his presence spooked him. He
still wore the pale, sick pallor of one confronted by
unearned & undeserved & unexpected frontal nudity.

"You believe me now?" asked Gabriel. Michael
couldn't articulate words. He nodded, still somewhat
paralyzed from his peculiar experience with Jessica,
whom he bizarrely exploded. "So what happened?" Gabriel
asked.

Michael tried to shrug, but even that required
effort. He spoke like a frazzled witness reporting a
hideous crime that had happened too quickly to a police
officer. "I don't know! I was just in the
fieldhouse..." he said, shaking his head, "and then
some girl I used to know came up to me and asked me to
go alone with her to the library--"

"You didn't lay with her, did you?" interjected
Gabriel.

"Lay with her?" asked Michael, confused and
irritated.

"Lay with her. Like from the Old Testament?"
clarified Gabriel. After a moment, he gestured
intercourse.

"--No!" Michael replied. "I mean, she tried, but when we got there she exploded! She exploded right in front of me and turned into a bunch of bugs!"

Gabriel nodded, intrigued but not particularly surprised by the outcome of his story.

"I killed her!" Michael said to himself, wringing his hands through his hair. "I killed the only girl to ever show me her boobs."

"She was never a girl, Michael," Gabriel corrected him. "She was a demon."

This didn't register well with Michael. "What do you mean?"

"Do you remember how you did it?" Gabriel pressed. "How you exploded her?" Though Michael was the prophesied one, the angel still wasn't sure precisely what class of superpower he possessed.

"I don't remember," Michael replied. "She was clawing at me and I just tried to get her off of me."

"How? What did you do to her?"

Michael shook his head. "I don't know. It all happened so fast. The last thing I remember was telling her that we should just be friends."

"Huh," mused Gabriel. "In English?"

Michael didn't understand the question nor did he care to consider it. "Gabe, what the hell is going on?"

Gabriel sat down as if what he were about to say was physically heavy and he couldn't hold it. "Do you know the story of the angel Lucifer?" asked Gabriel. Michael shook his head. He had hardly been taught the content of the Federalist Papers, much less religious apocrypha that was expressly forbade by the State Board of Education.

"Lucifer was an angel of Heaven, like me," said Gabriel. "But one day he got it into his head that he should be the one in charge. So he plotted a coup to wrest the Kingdom of Heaven from God. Now the rest of us were like, 'Don't be an idiot. We've got a good thing going on.' And he was like, 'No, it'll be awesome.' Then some stuff about panties and pony kegs or something. Well God finds out, and it turns out that God doesn't want to have the Kingdom of Heaven wrested from him, so he expelled Lucifer for all of eternity."

Michael stared blankly. "And so he sent him to Hell?" asked Michael.

"Not really," Gabriel responded. "Lucifer chose to reside in Hell. It's sort of like moving into the basement and stringing up blacklights and stuff."

Michael reprised his blank stare, an ostinato of annoyed dubiety.

"At any rate, Lucifer never stopped plotting to conquer his own paradise. You know, 'cause the basement's like damp and stuff and has spiders? So now, every one thousand years, Lucifer attempts to seize control of the earth and sow discord and chaos and sin, from which he might finally reconquer the heavens."

Michael blinked. "So what does that have to do with me?" he asked.

"Tonight is one of those nights, and you're the one who was prophesied to stop him." Gabriel shrugged as if it were as simple as that.

Michael frowned skeptically. "He's going to conquer Heaven from Crescent Lake High School?"

Gabriel shrugged again. "Yeah."

"I'm fourth on the depth chart," Michael protested. "I don't even get put in on nickel packages. What do you mean 'prophesied?'"

"I'm not sure. I only know that you're the only one who can stop him. That's why all those girls who come on to you are out to get you. If you have sex with them, you'll become unholy and therefore unable to stop Lucifer."

"So everyone else in the building is going to get to have sex tonight but I'm not allowed?" asked Michael.

"Pretty much."

Michael rubbed his eyes. "Where is this prophesy you're talking about?"

"It's in the Bible," replied Gabriel.

"Where?" demanded Michael.

"I don't remember. Somewhere toward the back," Gabriel said. This was not a satisfactory response for Michael.

"Have you ever read the Bible?" Gabriel asked rhetorically. "It's basically unreadable. Just a bunch of cryptic rules. And there's no narrative development whatsoever. Reading it cover to cover? Forget about it. It makes no sense. It's like a German war cipher."

Michael looked away, suddenly haunted by the image of Jessica's explosion into a cloud of locusts. This Lucifer stuff didn't make sense to him, but neither did Jessica's hideous, abrupt transformation. He paced and stared off into space, sort of like Marty McFly in Back

to the Future when he learns the natural scarcity of
1.21 gigawatts of electricity.

"You said that everyone who gets laid tonight is
going to birth a demon baby?"

Gabriel nodded. "Well, just a demon. Not a 'demon
baby.' That's not a thing." Gabriel chuckled at the
absurd notion of a demon baby.

"So what am I supposed to do? Keep everyone in the
building from having sex?"

Gabriel shook his head. "The demons are incidental.
Don't worry about that. If you stop Lucifer, you stop
the demons."

"So how do I stop Lucifer?" Michael heard himself
say the words but still couldn't believe he had arrived
at a moment in his life that would require him to say
that.

"Lucifer's here tonight because he's looking for the
most virtuous girl in school."

"Virtuous?" asked Michael.

"Chaste."

"Chaste?"

"Chaste. Celibate. I don't know how you say it in
20th century teenager." Gabriel sighed. "He's looking
for the one girl in your school who's the least likely
to put out."

Michael tilted his head. "Why? What's he want with
her?"

"To sleep with her."

"Of course!" Michael exclaimed, his frustration
turning to anger. "Everyone but me is allowed to hook

up tonight! Why not even the most chastey girl in school, too?"

"Relax, Michael," reassured Gabriel. "It won't be that easy. He's going to have to earn this one. Hopefully, that will give you enough time to find her and protect her until dawn."

"What do you mean?"

"If Lucifer can't complete his mission -- bedding this young woman before the sun rises -- then none of this happens. No demons. No Armageddon. No End of Days."

"It'll be like nothing happened?"

"Mostly. I mean, your classmates will remember that they boned each other. Monday will be awkward! And all the girls who do get pregnant will all have heavy periods." Gabriel frowned, remembering his ancillary janitorial duty. "That part will probably be pretty gross."

"When's dawn?"

"07:27am," said Gabriel.

Michael looked down at his loaned watch. There were hours upon hours ahead of him. He looked back at Gabriel. "I don't get it. If there's so much at stake, why doesn't God just come down and sit on Lucifer's face? Why does it have to be me?"

"God created the universe in six days like a zillion years ago. Sure, every once in a while, he'll show up to give everyone fish, or cater a wedding, but other than that, he doesn't really get involved."

Michael's expression indicated that he was still not satisfied with this arrangement. Gabriel didn't acknowledge it. He was preoccupied, testing a hand-held two-way radio, the kind with which janitors were always paging each other, as if they were coordinating the D-Day invasion every time someone threw up during final exams or that one day when the beef stroganoff didn't reach an internal temperature of 165 Fahrenheit.

Gabriel turned. "Michael, who's the most celibate, most prudiest girl in the school?"

Michael responded immediately, as if it were the easiest riddle ever posited to him. "Churchy Girl."

"Churchy Girl?" asked Gabriel.

"Sure. I don't remember her real name. But she's a prude. She's always going on and on and on about Jesus."

"Jesus." Gabriel considered this. Michael realized something important.

"Plus she's here with some old guy!"

Gabriel wasn't completely convinced, but this seemed to be a fair lead.

"Find her," he demanded. "Take her somewhere safe, somewhere away from everyone else. After that, I want you to contact me on this radio."

"Why can't you come with me?" asked Michael, accepting the two-way but reluctant to do it alone.

"You're the prophesied one, Michael. You're the one who has to do it. I will, however, help you. Just make sure to contact me on that radio."

Michael frowned. Is this what made him the prophesied one? The knowledge that Churchy Girl was churchy? Everyone knew that. So why'd it have to be him? His silent complaint was interrupted.

"Why do you keep doing that?" asked Gabriel.

"Doing what?" Michael asked. He didn't realize he had been periodically hiking his dress pants. Gabriel pointed to his sagging slacks.

"Oh. One of the, er, demons took my belt."

Gabriel took a moment to visually tailor him. He turned to a thin steel cabinet, its paint cracked and faded near the hinges and sides, and took out a short, 2½ foot bungee cord, the kind that was typically used to secure small loads on vehicles or bind unwieldy packages. Gabriel wrapped it through the loops to secure his pants, a makeshift belt.

"Okay," said Gabriel, like a captain addressing a paratrooper at the proper altitude. "You're ready."

Michael disagreed that a bungee cord around his waist was adequate preparation for the task that lay ahead of him, a task he neither wanted nor asked for.

"Go get her," said Gabriel. "Take her someplace safe. Then contact me on that radio. I'll take care of everything from there."

Michael looked at the red line on Gabriel's vandalized clock with reluctant curiosity and sighed. He had climbed the wrong depth chart.

Churchy Girl and her date, whose liberal use of gel
product seemed to emphasize rather than disguise the
early thinning indicators of hair loss, danced
playfully close on the dance floor. There was an
unusual chemistry between them, the creepy kind that
one might find between a church youth group leader and
his favorite pupil. They were both unaware that Michael
Williams, who had already ruined the Homecoming game,
was surveilling them from the mezzanine over the court.
He found their proximity disaffecting and creepy, but
it, combined with his advanced age and her reputation
for New Testament moralities, helped to reassure him
that he had found Lucifer and his unsuspecting target.

Rubber bands, thought Michael. This would require rubber bands. Before Edwin McCain had finished serenading the strands in her eyes, Michael had returned to his observation deck in the mezzanine -- which now became a demon-hunting blind -- with a plastic bag of seven-inch rubber bands. He loaded one onto his finger and fired it with prejudice at Churchy Girl's date.

It went wide right.

He re-loaded and tried again.

It went wide left.

He took another rubber band and fired again.

It sailed over both their heads. Fortunately no one else on the dance floor had yet noticed the salvo of angry, multi-colored rubber being fired from the heralded sniper above.

Michael lined up the fourth band. "Our Father, who art in heaven," he muttered to himself, "hallowed be Thy name..." He ripped the fourth band. This one was true to its target, striking the evil suitor, verily the Devil incarnate, in his left eyeball.

"Ow!" the imposter exclaimed, immediately pressing his hands to his eye. He had no idea what had just accosted him, but it stung like a bitch. As Churchy Girl rushed to his side to see whether he was okay, Michael jumped the railing that separated the mezzanine from the lower deck and shimmied down the stacked bleachers, impressed with his own action movie agility. Maybe he was meant for greatness after all.

Before Churchy Girl could ascertain whether her date was okay, Michael had grabbed her by the wrist and

tugged her away. She resisted at first, but Michael
shouted "it's contagious!" and Churchy Girl acquiesced
in profound confusion.

Moments later he had led her, despite her protests,
to the girls' locker room that was housed within the
fieldhouse. It was windowless and secure, almost
bunker-like, and could protect its occupants from a
wide gamut of dangers, from tornadoes to voyeurs to
Lucifer himself. Or so Michael hoped.

He threw the deadbolt lock behind him.

"We should be safe here," he said. He was both
informing her and reassuring himself.

"What are you talking about? Safe from what?" asked
Churchy Girl.

"Safe from your date!" replied Michael. "Do you have
any idea who that guy is?"

"Yeah," she said flatly, annoyed. "He's Eric
McMahon."

"Who?"

"Eric McMahon." Michael's blank expression demanded
she elaborate. "He was a senior when we were in eighth
grade."

"Eric McMahon?" Michael scoffed. "More like
LUCIFER!"

Churchy Girl frowned, her eyes scanning her
exercised peer and narrowing cautiously over a Motorola
radio he had clipped to his bungeed pants for some
reason. "Have you been drinking?"

"Yeah, I've been drinking," replied Michael.
"Drinking up the Apocalypse! Listen, Churchy Girl--"

"That's not my name. Stop calling me that. My name is--"

"--that guy is the fallen angel Lucifer and he's only here for one reason and one reason alone." Michael paused dramatically so as to offer her a moment to gather herself before inundating her with the true, horrible reason behind "Eric's" occurrence at the dance.

"He's here to get on top of you."

Churchy Girl rolled her eyes at him. "Well duh. Why do you think I invited him?"

Michael hesitated. This was not the response he anticipated.

"He's a college guy!" Churchy Girl continued. "He's experienced!" Michael looked at her sideways as she derisively added, "Why'd you come to the dance tonight? For the ambiance?"

There was a long pause as Michael considered this information. "Wait, you want to sleep with him?" he asked.

She rolled her eyes. "You're so naive. This is why I can't date high school boys."

"I thought you were all churchy and chaste and virtuous," appealed Michael.

"God wants us to be happy."

"Not me apparently," grumbled Michael.

Churchy Girl stood and went for the exit. "So is that that? Are we done now?"

Michael snagged her by the arm. "Wait! Just listen to me for two more seconds. I know this sounds crazy, but if you lose your virginity to that guy tonight, the whole world is going to end, okay?"

She laughed at both the absurdity of the statement and its premise. "Very noble, Michael. But if that's what you're trying to protect me from, you're too late."

A wave of panic washed over Michael. "You didn't!"

She smiled. "I did. Vacation Bible School, summer after eighth grade. Not that that's any of your business."

Michael paused, confused. He struggled through the arithmetic. "...So you're not a virgin?"

"Want to stick your hand up there and find out?"

Michael turned away from her like during those dramatic moments in soap operas. "Oh my God...," he began.

"Don't blaspheme," she interjected.

"...if you're not the most virtuous girl in school, then who is?"

She started for the door, leaving Michael sitting on a heavily lacquered pine bench, but paused as she reached the door. She turned and looked at him in a peculiar manner, her mind reconstructing the valiant assault. "Did you really shoot him with a rubber band?"

"Huh?" asked Michael. He was lost in the task ahead of him, which was now made so much more daunting.

"Did you shoot Eric in the eye with a rubber band?"

Michael shrugged his confession. "Yeah...?"

She looked at him differently. In a perverse way, this flattered her. She studied him for a moment before telling him, "If he can't deliver because of this, I'm coming to find you." She unlocked the door and left.

"Deliver what?" Michael asked aloud as the door closed behind her.

Michael sat, alone, in the girls' locker room. He was unsure of whether she'd return to yell at him or seize what he had callously stolen from her. Both options discomfited him.

Michael exited the girls' locker room having attempted little and already out of ideas. The only good lead he had for Most Chaste of Crescent Lake had turned out to be among its Least. Less so than even Reghan Weaver, perhaps. He took a good long inventory of the fieldhouse and the hundreds of people in it, overwhelmed by the task of locating either Lucifer or his intended. He was ready to grasp at straws.

He was always ready to grasp at straws.

He struggled to identify anyone he might not recognize or might otherwise strike some kind of red flag. Among the hundreds there who might be the unidentified villain and victim, a particular couple stood out, a boy and girl, engaging in what appeared to be an unpleasant discussion. Maybe this was them.

As he crossed the room to extemporaneously interrogate them, the girl turned her back to the boy and stormed off. Michael approached the suspect in a manner he would have described as gallant. Anyone else would have called it belligerent. Schizophrenic even.

"Hey you!" he called.

The boy heard him but did not react.

"Are you Lucifer?" he asked him.

"What?"

"Never mind. Who was that girl you were talking to?"

"My sister," he replied, confused by the tone of the question.

"What were you guys arguing about?"

"None of your business," said the brother. Michael hesitated. So far the story checked out. He pressed further, however, the urgency of his mission demanding thoroughness.

"Does she put out?" Michael asked. The subtle touch of Peter Falk he did not have.

"What?" asked the brother.

"I said, 'Does she put out?'"

The brother narrowed his brow in a look of hostility that most simians would've understood, giving Michael one final opportunity to explain himself. Michael forfeited it.

"C'mon, man, it's important. Is she easy? I need to know!"

The impatient brother defended his sister's honor with a fist, an awkward jab that caught Michael's face. No further verbal response was necessary, and no chaperone was present to prevent the act of vigilantism. By the time Michael had righted himself, the brother was gone and the sister, perhaps exonerated though not explicitly, even more gone.

Michael winced, rubbed his eye, and glanced through his injury around the fieldhouse. There were hundreds of people here, many he knew but still more he didn't.

This was already a bad plan, he concluded. Interviewing everybody in the school about their sexual proclivities would take forever and expose him to more violence. Better to address them all at once.

Michael sprinted up to the stage, leaped onto it, and seized the DJ's idle microphone. He flipped the power switch before anyone could notice.

"Everyone," he yelled into the microphone, "stop dancing! I have an announcement!" The student body attempted to ignore him, but Michael continued. "I'm serious! Listen to me! It is very important that no one here has sex tonight!" The crowd, rejecting both his annoying interruption and his dictum, turned against him. A chorus of boos rained down on him like a sudden spring hailstorm. "You will all have demon babies that will enslave us at dawn!" The boos only grew louder. "Well, not demon babies," Michael corrected himself. "Just regular demons, which are actually worse!"

Someone threw an empty flask, which clocked him in the forehead, leaving an impressive gash. Michael, however, was undeterred. "I'm serious! This is important!" he shouted over the booing. "It's the end of the world! I know this for a fact -- the janitor told me so!" The student body continued jeering in operatic reprise.

Ms. Fulmer, the attractive student teacher who had until this point been absent and uninterested in the goings-on of the evening, arrived at the base of the two-foot stage to both assist Michael in his head injury and disarm him of the microphone.

"Get down here, Michael," she said, sternly but not necessarily coldly.

"I can't, lady!" Michael protested into the microphone. "Lucifer's looking for play and I've got to stop him!" Somewhere, Churchy Girl rolled her eyes.

"What?" Ms. Fulmer asked incredulously.

"I know it sounds crazy, but someone here is in imminent danger!" He continued speaking into the microphone for some reason. "From Lucifer!"

"Who's in 'imminent danger'?" asked Ms. Fulmer skeptically.

"I don't know!" he yelled again into the microphone as the DJ tugged it from his hand. Ms. Fulmer pulled him off the stage and ushered him back toward the locker rooms, where Michael was only moments ago. One step forward, two steps back.

"Michael, are you okay?" she asked with a surprising level of compassion.

"I know it sounds crazy, but Lucifer is here tonight and he's trying to get on the most chaste girl in school so that he can destroy the world."

"Have you been drinking?" she asked.

"No."

"Drugs?"

"No."

Ms. Fulmer stopped abruptly and examined Michael for signs of head injury. She focused on each pupil, looking for asymmetrical dilation.

"Lucifer from the Bible," he clarified.

She nodded, humoring him, manipulating his face and discovering no indication of concussion.

"Yeah, I know that sounds dumb," he conceded, as she
led him into the athletic trainer's office that was
adjacent to the fieldhouse. It was the closest thing to
a medical facility in the school, windowless and
sterile. She flipped the lights. It was bright like a
surgical suite, revealing two examination tables that
had seen nothing worse than a few sprained ankles in
the short history of its operation. Posters on the wall
indicated instructions for wrapping particular sports
injuries. Lay-ups that went wrong or digs that weren't
properly dug.

She pushed him onto the first examination table.

"This really isn't necessary," he said.

"Sit still," she replied, as she tore open a pad of
gauze and applied it to his bleeding forehead. She
showed him the pad, and even he was surprised at the
prodigious amount of blood it had bled.

"Yeah but seriously, though, I have to go," he
pleaded, trying to stand. She shoved him back down with
both hands like an ER physician restraining one who
lacked the authority to release himself against medical
advice.

"Michael! Please! Sit still," she demanded. Michael
had no recourse but to lift his legs onto the table in
order to keep balanced. She leaned over him again, this
time with a tube of gel and a butterfly bandage.
Michael paused, unused to any female making such
specific physical demands against him, particularly
from one who had accidentally deprived half of the
student body of academic instruction. Despite her
thorough insight into tone & style & subtext of 19th

century American literary canon, the boys in her classes were uniformly more focused on her fuzzy Angora sweaters. He sat perfectly still and considered the odd singularity of this moment.

Surely the last male to be within this distance of her generous bust was over 21. Not only could he purchase his own liquor, but he probably only shopped those with fancy labels or unpronounceable names, serving them in the proper glassware vessels that he had never seen at any of the juvenile, bottom-shelf summer binges he had attended. This guy surely had his own car. His own lease on his own apartment. Fake yet passable tropical fauna. Ironic damask. Ramekins. He was probably in grad school and spoke two languages--

Michael had always underestimated himself.

Ms. Fulmer crossed the room to open a drawer and locate additional first aid. Michael was distracted by his own suddenly-arisen feelings of severe inadequacy, comparing himself to this other suitor he had invented on her behalf, according to preferences he had assumed that she held.

He jerked himself up, trying to escape the inadequacy and remembering his mission to locate the imperiled, prophesied girl who required his attention. Ms. Fulmer shoved him back down.

"You're still bleeding," she gently reprimanded. She was quick, efficient. "And we don't want you losing any more blood." Michael hesitated. What the hell did that mean? While he explored the cryptic nature of the sentence, she crossed the room and removed an ice pack from a freezer chest.

"Put this on your eye," she insisted. He did as he was told and pressed it against the bruise that was forming on his face, his punishment for inquiring about a sister's sex life from sister's brother.

"How do you feel?" she asked.

"Fine...," he responded in a cautious manner that would have persuaded no one that he was actually fine.

There was a desk lamp in the corner with a conventional incandescent light bulb. The athletic trainer, who kept limited hours, preferred the warm, subdued light to the harsh fluorescents, particularly when there were no ankles to wrap or shins to ice. Ms. Fulmer swapped the lighting, killing the fluorescents and firing the homey lamp. The room suddenly had the queer intimate feeling of a college dorm room, not that Michael had any experience in that kind of environment.

"Is this better?" she asked.

"I don't know," he said, afraid to commit to anything, no matter how inconsequential.

She removed her long, wide, 63% cotton 37% polyester scarf and draped it over the lampshade, further muting the 60-watt bulb and diffusing a cool, hushed blue into the room. "How about now?" she asked quietly, her décolletage now conspicuously exposed.

No, this was worse. But Michael pleaded the fifth. "I don't know," he said again.

There was a long pause while she evaluated him, but she was no longer making medical diagnoses. Michael felt extremely self-conscious.

"I know what you think about in English class, you know," she said to him.

"You do?" he said cautiously. Mostly he just thought about being hungry. His English class was right before lunch. But he'd be lying if he said he had never cheated on Emmaleigh by imagining what was under the student teacher's snug fitting camisoles.

She stared him down for a moment.

"Would it make you feel better if you could see them?" she asked.

Michael dropped the ice pack. Surely this was a trap, he thought, a joke or an elaborate cruel prank that required her to flirt with committing a felony. He didn't get it at all.

"I'm sure some Tylenol will be sufficient," he said, trying to shrug but unable to complete the gesture with his back pressed against the table.

She showed him anyway, wrapping her arms across her abdomen and peeling her camisole over her head. She added it to the perfume-scented scarf that was already draped over the lampshade. She stepped closer to him, reached behind herself, and removed her bra.

"What do you think?" she asked, dropping it to the floor.

Michael was, predictably, unable to speak. These were the largest breasts he had ever seen. To be fair, he had only seen four. And even that wasn't such an impressive number. It turns out that they come in pairs. The bilateral symmetry of vertebrates, he recalled from a biology lecture. The textbook had hardly prepared him.

He averted his eyes, racking himself for an adjective. "They're... they're... good," he concluded, somehow equivocally, his voice accidentally cracking. "They're very good."

She looked at him, drawing the faintest thin smile. It bordered on a smirk. She was playing with him. Cruelly, she unbelted her slacks and allowed them to fall to the floor.

Michael appealed to divine entreaty. "Hail Mary, full of grace, the Lord is with thee, blessed art thou among women..." he started under his breath.

"What are you doing?" she asked indifferently.

"I'm just... praying," he said.

"Is it coming true?" she asked, untying his shoes and discarding them. She was still behaving like an ER physician, efficiently cutting through clothes that were obstacles to treatment. He didn't answer her question.

"I want to hear you say it out loud," she quietly demanded. "When you see me in class, what do you think about?" There was a teasing tone to her voice, but still one that demanded a verbal response.

"Um..." Michael politely replied.

The volume of her voice lowered as she got closer to him. "Do you think about seeing me naked?" she asked, and with that she removed her remaining underwear and was completely unencumbered.

He scratched his forehead uncomfortably and tried to avert his eyes, looking toward the ceiling.

"Do you think about me wrapping my mouth around you?" she asked, her hand now groping him in the area she had implicitly referenced.

He felt cotton-mouthed. He couldn't swallow. It was getting hard to breathe. Somehow this was worse than his first middle school athletic physical, when he had been disrobed, probed, and asked to cough. He coughed now, trying to clear his throat.

"Do you think about calling me by my first name while you penetrate me?" she asked, climbing on the examination table and straddling herself over him. Michael remained motionless underneath her, wishing himself invisible. He didn't say anything.

She leaned into him, her D-sized endowment brushing along his chest, then face, and whispered into his ear. "So what do you think about when you look at me in class?"

She rose over him, arching her back. He stole a long glimpse of her, the generously proportioned older woman whom every boy in the class had imagined in exactly this situation. Completely nude. Efficiently conducting the lesson here as she did in class. Awaiting the green light. It occurred to him that she was waiting for an answer.

He told her the truth, the embarrassing, shameful truth, but somehow it came out again in a language that he insisted he could not speak:

"Prandiu. Ego cogito de cibo."

And with that, Ms. Fulmer, so tragically close to receiving her Bachelor's of Science in Education, exploded into a cloud of locusts.

"Jesus Christ!" Michael exclaimed, covered for the second time tonight in a thick cloud of bugs that used to be a buxom nude female who was willing to go all the way. He scrambled to his feet, shuffling the bugs off of him, and bolted for the exit. He threw the door closed behind him and pulled with all of his weight against the handle, as if whatever was sealed inside might try to release itself. He didn't even care that his shoes were still in the room, or that he left an incandescent light burning on the other side. Energy conservation was not a top priority at this moment. He had just witnessed the second girl who had ever exposed herself to him explode into a cloud of bugs. Was this going to happen every time, for the rest of his life?

He was then reminded of the thing that Gabe said, the thing about every girl who came onto him being a demon. Had the student teacher been a vicious demon this entire time, whose two roles at the school were 1) to facilitate a Socratic discussion of the common themes in the required summer reading list and 2) to completely & utterly destroy Michael on this precise cursed night?

He returned to the fieldhouse where he again took a panicked inventory. His eyes darted around the room as he tried to devise a new plan. Mounted on an adjacent wall was a fire alarm, and he decided to go nuclear. The bells would surely drive everyone from the building, including Lucifer's pursued, chaste paramour. At the very least it would buy him some time.

He raced to the red lever and, without regard to the many witnesses in the room, grasped the handle and threw it like a vindictive prison executioner condemning the guilty to electric absolution.

But nothing happened.

It didn't ring.

It didn't alarm.

Of course it didn't, Michael thought. What it did do, however, was spray his hand with green ink, something the alarms were designed to do in order to tag the reprobates who molested them for no reason.

"God damn it!" he cursed in response.

"Dude, what are you doing?" asked a familiar voice. Michael turned to find Kody behind him. Before Kody could ask why Michael was throwing fire alarms or

seemed to be suffering a blackened eye, Michael yelled
at him.

"Kody! Where have you been?"

"What do you mean? Why are you pulling the fire
alarm?" Kody asked. "And Jesus, what happened to your
face?"

Michael ignored the question. "I've got something
important to tell you," he said, frazzled.

"Me too," Kody grinned. "Do I look like a man,
Mike?"

"No, you look like an asshole! I've been looking for
you for like an hour!"

"Why, what's wrong?" asked Kody, reading the heavy
pallor on Michael's face. "Is it your syphilis?"

"Shut up. You know about Lucifer, right? Like from
the Bible?"

"It is your syphilis," Kody mused, delivering the
diagnosis.

"Knock it off!" interjected Michael.

"Okay, fine, what about Lucifer?"

"He's an alumnus of our high school apparently and
he's--" Michael stopped abruptly. "Wait a minute. What
do you mean, 'Do I look like a man?'"

Kody grinned a shit-eating grin. "Jordyn and I went
all the way! I got a boner and we had sex!" He threw up
his palm for an unrequited high-five.

"Oh, shit," Michael replied. He brought his green
hand to his forehead, smearing a tiny bit of ink
against his temple. "How you could do that?" he asked
in increasing panic.

"Just like Mrs. Fuchs taught us in health class. The blood flowed to the penis, I put it in the vagina, and like eleven seconds later--"

Michael shook his head. "I didn't mean physically!"

"It was awesome," admitted Kody. "I think everyone should do it."

"Everyone IS doing it! That's the problem!" protested Michael.

Kody put on his best-friend face and patted a kind hand on Michael's shoulder. "Don't be so hard on yourself, Mike. It'll happen for you someday, when you're ready. And with the right girl. And the corpora cavernosa fills with venous blood and makes your wiener hard."

"I've been with TWO of the right girls tonight and I exploded them into bugs!"

"What?" asked Kody.

"Ego anathema," he said to himself, tugging at his hair again.

"Why do you keep doing that?" asked Kody, frustrated.

"Exploding girls? I have no idea! It just happens!" Michael exclaimed, wishing he had some control over his unusual, burdensome superpower.

"I don't even know what you mean when you say that," said Kody. He was teasing about the syphilis, but there was definitely something about Michael that was unbalanced. Kody clarified, "I meant speaking in weird languages."

Michael paused. He heard Gabe's voice echo in his head: "I said we should just be friends," Michael had said, to which Gabe had replied, "In English?"

Michael dropped to a chair underneath the festive blue & silver balloons and stared, open-jawed, into space. That's when Jordyn found them. Her dress was smartly put back together; her hair was a post-coital fuss.

"What's wrong with him?" she asked Kody, referring to Michael. "Where are your shoes?"

Michael looked at her abdomen and sighed.

The Most Evil Kind of Pregnant

"Yup, you're definitely pregnant," Gabriel said to
Jordyn. "Pregnant in high school: the most evil kind of
pregnant." He was examining her as she sat on a
workbench in the boiler room. Michael sat in the
corner; Kody paced in alternating states of disbelief &
skepticism & denial.

"I told you to stay away from that girl!" exclaimed
Kody to Michael, as if the perfunctory advice would
have prevented Lucifer's pre-ordained siege of his alma
mater, 1000 years in the making.

"You told me she had hepatitis, not that she was a
demon sent to ruin Homecoming and destroy the world,"
Michael angrily rebutted.

Jordyn ignored the squabble. "What's going to happen
to me?" she implored Gabriel.

Gabriel frowned. "Well, one of two things. Either Lucifer finds his bride and consummates, in which case you'll gestate and deliver shortly after dawn, or Michael successfully thwarts Lucifer, in which case you'll just have an unusually heavy period... which will occur shortly after dawn. Either way," he said tactlessly, "it's going to be gross. If you've got some pads in your locker, you might want to think about grabbing them."

Kody and Jordyn both looked at him with categorical incredulity.

Gabriel continued. "Then, of course, comes the war, famine, and inflation."

"Inflation?" asked Kody.

"This is stupid," concluded Jordyn in a manner that suggested that should she refuse to believe it, it would cease to be true. Kody nodded in accord and reached his hand out to assist Jordyn off the table after her creepy, reluctant obstetrical examination by the guy who mopped up spaghetti every other Tuesday.

"That's fine. I don't need you to believe me," said Gabriel. He turned to Michael. "We're wasting time anyway. You're supposed to be out finding that one girl--" started Gabriel.

"No, wait," Michael interjected. "I need him to believe me. I need his help. You've got to convince them, Gabe."

There was a stubborn pause while Gabriel deliberated whether their assistance was necessary. But so long as it helped get Michael back to the arena, he assented.

"Okay," he said. "You want proof?"

Both Jordyn and Kody braced. They actually didn't want proof; they preferred the comfort of their skepticism. Gabriel pressed on.

"I've got it. You know how angels don't have genitals? Or shame or modesty?"

"No," answered all of the high schoolers, even Michael, in unison, afraid of where this was going.

"Well, we don't. See?" Gabriel unbuttoned his gray jumpsuit and dropped trou.

"What the hell are you doing?" cried Kody, averting his eyes. Jordyn sat dumbfounded as Gabriel exposed his shorn, G.I. Joe-like groin. This was alarming, but they were even more disturbed when Gabriel's angel parts lit up the room like a magazine cover photo shoot. He didn't have to keep himself revealed for long; they were convinced fairly quickly. Even Michael, who had already been blinded on his detour to Damascus, was bewildered by this conclusive evidence of Gabriel's divinity.

"Why wouldn't you have done that the first time I came in here!?" Michael demanded.

Gabriel shrugged. "I don't know," he said casually. "It didn't occur to me."

Michael sighed, annoyed. It seemed that Gabriel, for all his apocalyptic urgencies, had not planned out this ordeal as thoroughly as he could have.

Kody and Jordyn both sat dumbfounded for another moment as Gabriel rebuttoned himself. Kody finally found some words.

"Okay," he said, nearly catatonic, "I believe you."

Jordyn put her hands over her belly, a bit less reluctant to entertain the thought that she might be incubating a demon progeny.

"So who's the most virtuous girl in the school?" asked Kody, ready to aid in whatever way he possibly could. He didn't want to watch his girlfriend give birth to a demon that would enslave him.

"We don't know," replied Michael, to which Gabriel responded, "We don't?"

"No," said Michael. "It turns out that Churchy Girl is kind of a slut."

"Churchy Girl is a slut?" asked Kody, further dumbfounded. Nothing about tonight was making sense at all.

Jordyn interjected. "Wouldn't it be easier just to find Lucifer instead of whoever this girl is? I mean, when did he graduate? Couldn't we just find the guy his age?"

"No," replied Gabriel. "He's Lucifer. He can shift forms; he can possess bodies; he can change his appearances as he wishes. The first time I met him, he was a fig tree, okay?"

"Fig tree?" asked Michael.

"He tasted awful," said Gabriel, shying from the memory as if there were much more humiliation to it. So much more.

"Why wouldn't you have told me that before I accosted the only forty-year-old at the dance?"

"The point is, you can't find Lucifer, okay? He's everywhere and nowhere. He's ubiquitous."

"Ubiquitous?" asked Jordyn.

"Qmnipresent. In the background. All the time,"
explained Gabriel. "Like those AQL floppy discs you get
in the mail."

Kody gasped, horrified at the magnitude of Lucifer's
reach. They even disabled the overwrite capability on
those discs, rendering them completely useless. Lucifer
was everywhere and read-only?

"Forget about Lucifer," said Gabriel. "You guys have
to help me find this girl. That's it! It's as easy as
that! Do you have any idea who she could be?" He
grabbed last year's yearbook, the same one he had been
poring over when Michael had stumbled into his shop
much earlier. He opened to the Juniors' photo section
and passed it to Jordyn. "I already X'ed out all the
ones who aren't her." This explained the vulgar Sharpie
lines across several of the female classmates. There
were notes written in Latin alongside those who were
scratched out. Jordyn was surprised to find that her
photo was among those painted with the red X. She
pointed to the foreign script in the margin.

"What does this mean?"

"Um...," replied Gabriel. He didn't continue but his
body language suggested it might be a list of not
necessarily unflattering personal details that she
nevertheless wouldn't want recorded into some future Q
Gospel.

Kody was still wrestling with the situation. "This
doesn't make sense. If Lucifer could just possess
bodies, why wouldn't he just possess Michael's body and
then like stab himself or touch boobs or vaginas or
whatever it is that kills Michael?"

Michael bristled at the insinuation that achieving second base would slay him. Gabriel shook his head, losing patience.

"He'd have to get Michael to agree in some legally binding fashion, which Michael as the prophesied one would probably be incapable of doing."

"What do you mean?" asked Jordyn, ever skeptical but still pressing her belly, as if the pressure alone would cure herself of her imminent fate.

"Lucifer can't just usurp things. He cannot take what you don't offer or what you don't exchange. He's surprisingly very scrupulous. Very legal. All evil things make you sign contracts or otherwise find ways to bind you in your own consent. Why do you think the evilest people are drawn to law school?"

"Dude," said Kody, "My mom's a lawyer."

"She's probably evil," Gabriel demurred.

"This is stupid," said Jordyn, renewing her protest. "If it's just about getting permission, I would never just--"

"No?" asked Gabriel? "Never bought eight CDs for a penny? Twelve for the price of one?" he asked rhetorically, almost smugly. Jordyn sat up, chagrined by her own burdensome subscription to evil that had saddled her with unpopular compilation albums. She began to rebut, but Gabriel sobered them with his lost patience.

"C'mon, we don't have time for this right now. Every minute, Lucifer gets closer to bedding this girl. And that's if he hasn't done it already."

A moment passed without argument.

Michael sat up. No one noticed that he had had an epiphany. "What constitutes a contract?"

Gabriel shrugged. "The typical things. A signature. A seal. An exchange of property. Chattel. Seven years of labor for your foxy cousin."

"Chattel?" asked Kody.

"How about a ring?" asked Michael.

"Eh. I suppose," said Gabriel. "Like a wedding band kind of thing? Engagement ring? Sure."

Michael looked off into space. "It's fate," he said to himself, inaudibly.

Kody saw Michael disappear into his thoughts. "Michael?" he asked, hoping he had stumbled into something useful. But Michael was momentarily unreachable, lost in a eureka moment. Kody, Jordyn, and Gabriel waited anxiously for Michael to share whatever had occurred to him.

"It's Emmaleigh," he confidently announced to the room. "And Cayden is Lucifer. He gave her his class ring. She's wearing it."

"Emmaleigh Davis?" asked Kody. "Are you sure?"

Michael looked back at him before deluging him with the overwhelming evidence. "I mean, why else would Cayden be interested in her? She never dates anybody, she doesn't put out, she's only worn a low-cut shirt twice in the last three years--"

"You've been monitoring that situation, have you?" asked Jordyn in a very judgmental tone. Michael ignored her.

"She's not 'hot', at least not in the superficial, conventional way. She's more like striking, you know? And special? The kind of special that--"

Gabriel interrupted him grimly. "You've got a thing for this girl, don't you?"

Kody answered for him. "You've got no idea."

Gabriel frowned. It was an intense frown. It indicated complication, that things might be worse than first appraised. "Now I get it," he said to himself, surprised and disappointed with himself that he could have missed something so, so obvious.

"Does that mean the contract has been fulfilled?" asked Kody.

"No," said Gabriel. "Not until consummation." Kody looked blankly at him. "Boning," elaborated Gabriel, gesturing crudely.

"We're running out of time," said Michael. "I need to find her now." He accepted that he wasn't very smooth with girls and solicited Jordyn's help. To locate Emmaleigh and her supernatural date this late in the evening required that he conscript a female perspective. "What doesn't Kody do that you wish he could?"

"What do you mean?" asked Jordyn.

"Is there anything that you wish Kody did for you that he doesn't?" asked Michael. He was polling her for clues as to what a typical high school girl might find alluring. Gabriel watched with interest as Michael assumed, without his realizing it, some position of agency. "Like what impresses you in a guy?"

She shrugged, searching for criticisms of her first serious boyfriend. She was able to summon several too quickly for Kody. "I wish he would dance with me," she said.

"Okay," that's good. He turned to Gabriel. "There's dancing in the gym, but they'd have to find someplace secluded, right?" Gabriel nodded in assent. He turned back to Jordyn. "What else?"

"I kind of wish he was smarter," she said. Kody raised his hands as if to say "what gives?"

"Yeah, okay, what else?"

"I wish he wouldn't burp the alphabet."

"That was one time!" interjected Kody.

"It was my grandparents' anniversary party."

"And I only got through F," he added in protest.

"No, c'mon. What have you seen other guys do that you wish he could?" Michael demanded.

She thought a moment longer and then realized it. "Oh," she said, "Once when I was hanging out at Baylee Lambert's house, her brother was playing the guitar and he was really good. And--" she stopped abruptly, suddenly too modest to finish the anecdote.

Michael gave an impatient shrug that demanded she go on. Kody grotesquely braced himself for the conclusion she was unwilling to share. Gabriel tried to jog her. "And...?" he asked.

"And I thought it was so hot that I ended up... sorta... going down on him."

Kody froze in horror. "I wasn't very good at it," Jordyn apologetically said to Kody, clumsily attempting to reassure him. It didn't.

"He didn't even--" Jordyn continued, but Kody refused to listen. He put his fingers in his ears and began loudly humming a very pained version of The Star Spangled Banner.

Michael & Gabriel ignored the rest. This was the answer they were looking for. "There's a grand piano in the auditorium."

Gabriel nodded. "That's it. Go get her."

Michael shook his head, deputizing the reluctant angel. "You're coming with me this time."

In 1994, the school district's electorate passed a millage that raised sufficient funds to build four new science classrooms, an auditorium (styled as the "Performing Arts Center"), and an Olympic-sized pool that the booster committee had hoped would attract state tournaments and subsequently tilt an advantage to the local swimmers & divers. There were also various giveaways to other athletic interests: new seed for the football field, improved tennis courts, brick pavers outside the track.

It was in this new Performing Arts Center that Lucifer, disguised as the heroic Cayden, had brought Emmaleigh to both separate her from the remainder of the student body and ply her with his seemingly boundless talent, both crucial elements of his plan to

lay her and subsequently achieve domination of Heavens
& Earth. His performance of Arabesque No. 1 was both
flawless and effortless, played with both
interpretation and precision, and the notes
reverberating from the grand piano were thrilling his
audience, comprised of Emmaleigh on the bench alongside
him, and, unbeknownst to him, Michael & Gabriel in the
engineered shadows of the catwalk above. They had snuck
into the auditorium without detection and were poised
above, ready to commence their plan. As soon as they
figured it out.

"Okay, tell me what to do," whispered Michael to
Gabriel, soliciting Plan A from his divinely assigned
angel, while Emmaleigh swooned below.

Gabriel shrugged, hesitant and uncertain. He seemed
to be anxious for an immortal creature. "I'm really
more of a wingman angel. And it's important that
Lucifer doesn't find out that I'm here."

"What do you mean?" asked Michael, feeling now twice
betrayed. "I thought you were supposed to help me!"

"I will help you," he said, hastening to add, "With
Emmaleigh. Not Lucifer. You're the prophesied one,
Mike, not me. This is your play."

"Are you serious?"

"Yeah. Besides, if Lucifer finds out that I'm here,
it's going to compromise our plan."

"Yeah, but we don't have a plan," replied Michael,
growing frustrated. "There's no plan to compromise!"

"Gabriel ignored his protest. "Plus, he's kind of a
dick. He's, like, really mean, and I don't want to have
to deal with it, you know?"

Michael started to wonder whether Gabriel was really
that valuable of an asset. "Isn't that why you're
here?" he pressed again.

"Trust me. I'm going to help you get everything
resolved. We're going to do this thing. But only as
soon as you can get Emmaleigh away from Lucifer."

"Yeah, but how do I get her away from him? That's
what I'm asking."

Gabriel raised his hands to indicate that it wasn't
his problem. "Wingman angel."

Michael just looked at him with frustration and
confusion, even contempt.

"Look, just go down there, get her away from him,
and then contact me on the two-way radio I gave you. I
have a plan that will take care of everything."

"Yeah," said Michael sarcastically, "'everything'
but the most important part! Like how I'm supposed to
pry her away from the guy she thinks is Cayden!"

Gabriel sighed. "You're the prophesied one, Mike.
I'm the--"

"Wingman angel." Michael completed his sentence.
"Right." He was having a hard time keeping his voice to
a whisper.

They were running out of time. Below, the boy
Emmaleigh knew as Cayden was completing the final dyads
of the movement. Based on her enthusiastic response,
the scheme was working. The final E reverberated
through the auditorium and faded into perfect silence.
Emmaleigh applauded with sincere enthusiasm.

"You have amazing hands!" Emmaleigh said.

"You have no idea," responded her date, who meant it
as a double-entendre. He dropped the keyboard cover
over the keys. It landed with a dull slam, a not-so-
subtle indicator that it was time to move onto Act III
of their night. He ran his hand through her hair,
tucking falling strands behind her ear. She resisted it
and embraced it at the same time.

He leaned in for the kiss and she capitulated. It
was gentle at first, but gradually became slightly more
intense, aggressive. He slid closer to her and
enveloped her with both hands. She feinted at pulling
away from him, and when his left hand groped her thigh,
she broke the kiss, laughing uncomfortably.

"I think maybe we should slow down," she said,
hoping he would agree. He paused, calculating the risk
of disobeying her, and then exhaled slowly, discharging
an annoyed sigh that he concealed from her. This would
require a lot of work. But the task demanded it. "So
what do you want to do now?" he asked.

She quietly re-opened the piano keys. "Keep
playing," she said. "I like it."

He stared back at her for a moment. It wasn't going
to be easy. He stole a subtle glance at his watch
before returning to the piano, he too aware of the
significance of 07:27am. But as he poised his fingers
back over the keys, he heard the sound of suppressed
male voices above him. He stole a glance at the catwalk
that hung in suspension 25 feet above them.

Michael was still demanding a more thorough plan
from his biblical advocate. And he still wasn't getting
it.

"'Go down there and get Emmaleigh' is not a plan," Michael angrily whispered to Gabriel.

"It is for you! You're the one."

Michael scowled.

"Just remember, contact me on the radio once you've gotten her," Gabriel added. This was the only component of the grand plan that he apparently was amenable to abet.

Below, Lucifer shook his head. He couldn't believe his luck. Maybe it wouldn't take a lot of work after all.

"What is it?" asked Emmaleigh.

His smile quickly receded as he faced Emmaleigh. He frowned and changed demeanor entirely. Whereas he was previously charming and polite, he was now suddenly cold, merciless. "I'm tired of playing footsie, Emmaleigh. This has to happen and it has to happen now." He advanced his hand up her leg and attempted to breach her dress. She resisted him.

"Cayden, wait," she protested. He didn't relent. With his free hand he grabbed the back of her hair, drew her violently closer to him, and kissed her neck.

"Please," she continued, "Cayden I don't want--"

He pulled away and looked her at coldly. "Emmaleigh, I know exactly what you want." She said nothing but her eyes pleaded with him to stop.

"Do you realize how lucky you are? Don't you know any other girl at this school would kill to be where you are?"

He was behaving uncharacteristically. This was not
the person she knew and had grown to know; she asked
his name aloud to test whether it was truly him.

"Cayden--?"

"We're alone. It's just us. No one's going to walk
in on us. Now shut up, unzip that shitty clearance-rack
dress, and let me do to you what you know you want me
to do to you." He again grabbed her around the waist
and again seized her dress between her legs.
Instinctively, she wound up and slapped him. Hard.

"Cayden" withdrew, intensely angry. After a brief
stand-off, he stood, an expression on his face so cold
it could freeze water. He looked her over sharply and
cut her as deep as he could.

"You fucking tease."

He turned quickly and walked out of the auditorium.
The impact of each step echoed across the empty rows of
seats, as the room had been extensively engineered to
do. Michael and Gabriel witnessed the fortuitous
forfeiture from the catwalk.

"See? This is our plan. Go get her," Gabriel said.
Michael sat for a moment, dumbfounded at the luck,
almost disturbed by it.

Emmaleigh remained at the bench, tears in her eyes,
unsure of what had happened or why he had suddenly
turned so cruel and unkind. But before she could begin
to audibly weep, indeed sob, a familiar face plummeted
down to the stage from the catwalk and landed without
grace in the net that hung over the orchestra pit. It
was designed to protect people from errantly walking
off the stage, not those intentionally diving from the

catwalk. It slowed him but not before he struck an
actual crash cymbal.

"Ouch," said Michael flatly as he climbed from the
pit, a small laceration on his upper arm from an
inopportunely placed orchestra stand.

"Michael?" asked Emmaleigh, surprised but not
alarmed. "What are you doing?"

He shrugged, played cool and nonchalant. "I thought
we might hang out."

She hugged him, intensely, tightly, relieved to see
a friend, someone who cared about her.

Yes, this seemed to be too easy. Michael was too
surprised to even properly hug her back.

Everything since the auditorium happened too easily, Michael thought. Emmaleigh didn't even insist on returning to the party in the fieldhouse after he quasi-rescued her. When Michael suggested they break into the faculty lounge together with his stolen janitorial key, she was not only amenable but excited about it. Whatever "Cayden" had said to her had driven her right to him.

The faculty lounge was a good hideout, Michael decided. At least temporarily. All of the classroom doorways had transom and sidelight windows, whereas the faculty lounge did not. Michael didn't know what went on in there or why the activities needed to be concealed, but he was pleased to have the privacy. And though he crushed on her with the unrestrained intensity of one thousand burning platitudes, he harbored no ungentlemanly designs. His priority was to protect her from her date, which at the moment didn't seem too difficult: right now she loathed Cayden. As they had walked to the faculty lounge, she had filled him in on his sudden change in temperament, how he had gone from gentleman to boor and how stupid she felt for falling for his obviously insincere long game. Michael wondered silently why he abandoned it so quickly but decided not to take such a gift for granted.

"Some guys are like that," he tried to reassure her. "Not all of them. But some of them."

They had talked for a little while before Michael became aware of the two-way Motorola radio that he had clipped inside his jacket. He had express instructions from Gabriel to contact him on that radio once they reached shelter. Michael groped for an expedient excuse to step outside and receive them. When he came up with one, he still ended it with a question mark, as if he himself didn't even buy it. As if he were disappointed and ashamed that he couldn't more easily summon a plausible excuse.

"I've got to go... smoke a cigarette?"

Instead of being annoyed by his peculiar evasiveness, she smiled at him. There was something oddly charming about him that only a day ago had been merely odd. "You're coming back, right?" she asked.

"Of course," he replied.

Maybe he was too embarrassed to tell her he was going to use the bathroom, she figured. She didn't know that Michael would never use a school bathroom unattended ever again.

He stepped out the door, too concerned with his
mission to even register her smile or consider its
meaning.

True, he left her alone and subsequently vulnerable
to an attempt by Lucifer to reacquire her, but somehow
it seemed a less perilous risk than taking her along
while he received instructions from the school janitor
about how to properly exorcise her. Were she to
overhear him talking with the janitor about how to
protect her from supernatural forces, she might be a
bit weirded out and less likely to stay in his company.
Besides, Gabe said that she had to consent, and
Emmaleigh was furious with "Cayden." Were Lucifer to
try to confront her again, she would probably wreak
some class of violence upon him.

Nevertheless, Michael attended to the task with
urgency. "We have to be quick, Gabe," he said over the
Motorola. "I left her in the faculty lounge. She's all
alone."

"You left her alone?" asked Gabriel. It was more of
a statement of dissent than it was a question. Michael
explained his reasoning to him; Gabriel conceded that
it made some sense.

"Besides," said Gabriel, reassuring them both, "Once
you take care of this, everything's going to be fine."

Michael continued down the long, dark B-wing hallway
as he had been instructed. "Where am I going?"

"Locker 213," replied Gabriel. In the janitorial
shop, Gabriel smiled. He was proud of this plan. It

made sense. It was going to ensure that Michael saved the world.

Michael didn't get it but did as he was told. There was something creepy about this, like he was Ripley in "Alien", as if the lockers contained live human beings frozen in suspended animation. He tried not to be a wuss but frequently looked over his shoulder.

"Okay, I'm there," said Michael, approaching a locker that was otherwise totally unremarkable. Gabriel relayed the locker combination to him, and Michael dialed it with deft precision, cautious that were he to make an error, the locker would explode and the world would end and Jordyn would expel a demon from her vagina and Emmaleigh would share a romantic moment with someone who wasn't him. Though he wasn't Catholic, he crossed himself before pulling the lever to open the locker door. No harm in covering bases. Besides, there was something about Gabe that Michael didn't find completely on the level.

Cold vapor escaped from the door as it opened, similar to that in the frozen food aisle at the grocery. It was thick, and the locker dark, but when it cleared and Michael shrugged off the chill, he found the locker to contain only one solitary item sitting on one solitary shelf:

A lonely, twenty-ounce bottle of a strawberry-flavored soda that was only available regionally, unimaginatively branded and artificially colored with fidelity to its name.

"Red Pop?" asked Michael skeptically into the Motorola.

"Yes," replied Gabriel. "This is extremely important, Michael. Make sure Emmaleigh drinks it. And whatever you do, don't drink any of it yourself."

"Why not?" asked Michael. But Gabriel didn't answer.

"Gabe, why not?" he asked again. Again he received no answer. He inspected the radio and found that the little red light was out. The battery had died. Shit.

Michael grabbed the pop bottle and slammed the locker shut.

Gabriel and Michael didn't know that their two-way radio band was a party line. Though Michael & Emmaleigh had long escaped the Performing Arts Center, Lucifer had remained in the auditorium and had found his way to the tech booth directly opposite from the stage. The booth, like the auditorium, was dark, but a tiny red light was remotely visible through the glass panes that lorded over the hundreds of empty seats facing the stage.

The light originated from a theater tech headset, the kind a stage manager might wear while trying to hustle players on and off the stage. Lucifer had tuned it to intercept Gabriel & Michael's conversation. He had been pleased with what he had heard so far.

"Michael? Michael, are you there...?" asked Gabriel over the radio. But Michael didn't answer. Lucifer

listened for the short burst of lonely static that
indicated their conversation was prematurely over.

He turned the headset off and removed the earpiece,
reclining in the high-back swivel chair and smiling
wryly. This wasn't part of his plan, but there was no
doubt it was fortuitous for him. And just at this
particular auspicious moment, a senior boy and his
junior date snuck their way into the darkness and
convenient solitude of the auditorium. They were having
a hard time keeping their hands off of each other.

Lucifer watched them approvingly, increasingly
confident in the inevitability of his victory at
daybreak.

When he returned to the faculty lounge where he had left Emmaleigh, she was still sitting at the table. She was looking down at the desk, spinning "Cayden's" class ring on the table like a top. She frowned at it, angry that it had been given to her under false pretenses and angry at herself for falling for it. She didn't know the half of it.

"Hi," he said, softly, to announce his return.

The ring dropped with an understated tinny clang. She turned to him and smiled. There was something genuine and authentic about it. It was the kind of smile that girls conceal from the world and use only for very consequential moments, so rare in fact that Michael didn't even realize he was seeing it.

"I brought you something," he said, clumsily offering her the pop bottle.

"Red Pop?" she asked, confused at the esoteric choice of beverage.

Michael shrugged. "I wanted to get you something. This is the best I could come up with."

After a moment she smiled. "Thanks," she said, but she didn't twist the cap. She just held the bottle in her hands. Michael watched it with grave intent. Gabe said that the bottle contained an antidote. All she had to do was drink the contents and maybe the next 1000 years would be preserved. He tried to telepathically convince her to open the bottle. But she instead set it down and spun the class ring again.

"How'd you know?" she asked without looking up to him.

"Huh?"

"How'd you know?" she asked again, this time making eye contact.

"How'd I know what?" The ring slowed and rotated to a rest on the table.

"Well, you were there. You knew he was going to try something and you were there for me. As soon as he was gone, you were there." She looked at him with what might have been some form of admiration as she lifted and spun the class ring on the table one more time. It rotated again in quick circles but this time it orbited toward the ledge of the table, where it lingered for a moment. But before it could recover from aphelion, it dropped from the table's edge and bounced quietly on the floor. Michael followed it, but Emmaleigh didn't. "How'd you know?" she asked again.

Michael surreptitiously extended his unshod foot
over the discarded ring before meeting her eye line.
"It just..." he started, not sure where he was going,
"The two of you?" He considered her question, paused
and willingly forgot his mission, suspending the
urgency of the several pressing tasks before him.
Looking at her there, it was just the two of them.
Somehow, suddenly, nothing else in the world mattered
or even existed. He spoke sincerely. His explanation
required no lie. "It just wasn't right."

Emmaleigh smiled at him, grateful to have him there.
She smiled and twisted the cap of the pop bottle as
Michael watched again with interest. She took a small
sip from the bottle, and Michael held his breath,
waiting for the verdict.

"This tastes different," she said, a bit
skeptically. Michael tensed. She sipped again. "It's
good. Do you want some?" she asked, offering him the
bottle.

Michael expelled his held breath, relieved, almost
ecstatic, but trying to restrain his sudden enthusiasm.
As far as he knew, this meant she was cured. Immune.

"No thanks," he politely said to her. She sipped
again.

"I don't really want to go back to the party yet.
You'll... you'll stay with me, right?"

Michael smiled. "Definitely."

                              Until Seven Thirty

    It was late. The dance was supposed to have
concluded hours ago. No one really seemed to mind,
however. Not McKenzie. Nor Mackenzie. Not even the DJ,
who had been given $2,000 in cash by the class
treasurer to play until seven-thirty AM. The remaining
chaperones, the ones who hadn't been reduced to
locusts, were nowhere to be found, all three pursuing
hobbies & endeavors afforded to them by the
supernatural occurrences of the evening.

    Lucifer, disguised as Cayden, now dateless but
nevertheless calm & relaxed, maneuvered through the
depths of the arena, examining the co-eds who had
discreetly come in and out of the fieldhouse throughout
the night. He could tell which of the girls were,
unbeknownst to them, carrying. It was a significant
number so far. He looked into the unencumbered faces of

the boys there who would soon become his slaves, all of
them gleefully ignorant of their imminent fates.
Everything was on schedule. Lucifer found himself
tapping his foot to the music.

He took a moment to consider the plight of his
rival. Somewhere in the building, Michael was clinging
to Emmaleigh, hoping Gabriel's plan would work.

Lucifer was hoping the same thing.

Lucifer knew Gabriel better.

Emmaleigh had finished the pop. Nothing remained of the beverage but a clear plastic bottle with a thin, syrupy residue and a modest ten-cent deposit.

Michael, meanwhile, was rifling through cabinets and drawers. Whatever he was looking for, he was failing to find it.

"What are you doing?" asked Emmaleigh.

"You wouldn't know where I could find some batteries, do you?" he asked, turning another drawer as if he were committing a hasty home invasion, intent on cash and jewels.

Emmaleigh stifled a laugh. It was an unusual laugh, perhaps the kind brought on by lack of sleep. She put her hand over her mouth in a manner suggestive of suppressing gossip.

"Yeah, I do," she said, removing her hand.

Michael paused. "Seriously?"

She nodded, a smile growing across her face. The smile broke into small fits of laughter. Michael didn't know what to make of this.

Nevertheless, Emmaleigh led them to Mrs. Fuchs' classroom not too far down the hall. It was a temple built for the spirited worship of the uterus & vas deferens, abstinence & contraception. The posters that hung on the wall, furnished primarily from the State Department of Health but some on loan from the teacher's private collection, illustrated testes and Fallopian tubes in peculiar, reverent detail. They may as well have been made of stained glass.

Emmaleigh maneuvered to the front of the room, where she slid open a drawer at the bottom of the teacher's desk. It was full of various battery-operated sex devices. Some of them were elegant in their minimalist forms; others were designed to resemble, well, the things they were supposed to resemble.

"Oh sick!" exclaimed Michael, after finally ascertaining their purpose. "Are these hers?"

Emmaleigh laughed again. "Every semester, Mrs. Fuchs separates the girls from the boys and teaches them about these things. Sometimes she asks us to write grant letters to the school board." She giggled before adding, "No one does."

Michael picked one of them up and handled it extremely delicately, not as if he were handling something fragile but rather out of some innate male fear that it might become provoked and sentient and force its way into his mouth or worse. He attempted to locate its battery but failed. Emmaleigh took it from him and retrieved the battery as smoothly as a firearms expert releasing a clip.

"Thanks," said Michael, deliberating whether he should feel threatened by her knowledge of the device. At any rate, he took the two-way radio from his pocket and prepared to swap the batteries.

"Hey," said Emmaleigh, rather abruptly. "Who was that girl you were dancing with earlier tonight?" She groped for words that would conceal a first-person singular pronoun. "...Some people were wondering."

"Oh," he replied dismissively. "You mean Lucy."

"What is her deal? Is she your date?"

He frowned, releasing the dead battery from the radio. "Not really. Turns out she only wanted me for my body and not my mind."

There was a pause while she evaluated him. "You're a good guy, Michael. I think you should be with a girl who knows that." Michael paused. She was being surprisingly candid for someone who had on Friday been somewhat evasive. If those incongruous positions bothered Michael, he either reconciled them or didn't care. This was the best opening she'd ever given him. Time to go for broke. He set the radio on the desk.

"I have something to admit to you," he said. "In fact, I already sort of did. I wrote it in a note that I hid in your chem notes, which I admit is pretty lame. But a certain course of events has happened tonight and convinced me that there really must be such a thing as fate and that we ended up like this, right here, right now, so that I could rectify that."

She looked at him curiously. His nerves began to
show.

"I've been afraid to say this to you for a long time
because every time I even just try to talk to you, I
just can't find words or I say something stupid or one
of your friends interrupts us or I get chased by a
yellow jacket, which I guess only happened one time,
but still..." He paused, catching himself. "But I guess
I usually just end up rambling awkwardly like I am
right now." He exhaled heavily and looked into her blue
eyes, clear and warm like shallow water. He forced it
out.

"Emmaleigh, I'm totally in love with you. I have
been ever since I saw you that first week of September
three years ago in Mrs. Morris' homeroom. I remember it
like it was yesterday. You were wearing this gray,
long-sleeved shirt with a green watch with a wide band
on it. Your hair was, like, tied back and kind of up,"
he gestured to illustrate it, "and you wore these
cuffed jeans with white sneakers and the kind of sock
that doesn't cover your ankle." Michael paused, unsure
whether his detailed memory of that moment was creeping
her out. But a thin smile drew across her face. She
remembered that shirt. She remembered that watch. The
smile grew broader as he elaborated.

"I remember thinking that you were really pretty,
like the kind of pretty I had never ever seen before
and haven't seen in anyone since. The kind that makes
you stop what you're doing. Or walk into desks and
knock over Tayler Stafford's social studies project
about Iraq." He grimaced. "I still don't know whether

you saw me do that. I hoped you hadn't." She released a
muted laugh.

"But what I remember most", he continued, "was
thinking that there was something about that moment
that was really important, like it was going to affect
my whole life. I remember thinking that I wanted to,
like--" he hesitated for a split second.

"I wanted to know what it was like to kiss you. Duh.
But even more than that I really just wanted to meet
you. I wanted to know everything about you. Things you
liked. Things you hated. Your favorite movies. Favorite
books. Your favorite color." He shrugged. "I wanted to
know what you did for fun and what you did after school
and what you thought about the world and whether I
could ever fit into yours." Michael was too self-
conscious to notice Emmaleigh smiling, sinking into her
own hands, intrigued that someone would hold on to a
moment like that so tightly. He continued, a chronic
inability to read the room. "And if you've ever even
remotely looked at me and wondered the same thing--"

But a moment like this called for action, not words.
Emmaleigh provided it.

She grabbed him by the collar and pulled him into
her, and they kissed. Passionately. The kind of kiss
that closes dozens of Golden Era Hollywood films. The
kind of kiss that Richard Wagner would set to opera and
Nazi propagandists would use to broadcast news of
eastern war triumphs. The kind of kiss that divides an
individual's otherwise long, volumed biography into
distinct epochs: everything before, everything
hereafter.

This was, succinctly, the best moment of his first seventeen years. The universe hinged on this exact place in space and time. It had reached an equilibrium. Nothing had or ever would make more sense than this.

After a moment, the kiss broke, though Michael was certain it would alter natural electromagnetic fields and reverberate into forever and cause planets on the edge of the solar system to oscillate aberrantly in their orbits. They looked into each other, borne into a new world. The old one would never look the same. But then Emmaleigh stumbled.

"I feel weird..." she said, "Dizzy." She put her hands to her head and listed as if she were subject to a peculiar, sideways gravity.

"...Are you okay?" asked Michael.

"I dunno," she said, slurring the words. She looked at him with profound, doped-up interest. "Kiss me again."

Michael hesitated. Something was wrong.

"Can you give me a sec?" he asked, standing.

She smiled, drunkenly, and nodded in a manner that flouted proper range of motion. Michael transplanted the batteries from the electric phallus into the Motorola.

He called up Gabriel.

Gabriel paced the custodial shop while Kody flipped idly through the marked-up yearbook and Jordyn silently tried to convince herself that she was in a peculiar dream. The radio crackled. Michael's voice came across it.

"Gabe, are you there?"

All eyes in the custodial shop darted to the radio. Gabriel raced to it.

"Michael!" answered Gabriel, relieved, "What happened?"

"The batteries in the radio died. I had to find new ones."

"Are you still with her?"

"Yeah, I'm with her, but--"

"Good. Did she drink that pop?"

"Gabe, something's wrong."

"What do you mean?"

"Emmaleigh just starting acting really weird out of nowhere."

Gabriel was undaunted. "Did she drink the pop?"

"Yeah."

Gabriel smiled. Michael couldn't see the smile over the radio, of course, but Kody & Jordyn both saw it and were comforted by it. They both exhaled in relief.

"Then it's fine," Gabriel said. "That just means the flunitrazepam is working."

There was a salient pause.

"The flewney-what?" asked Michael.

"The flunitrazepam," Gabriel replied.

"What are you talking about?"

"The Mickey you slipped her."

"What the hell is a Mickey? Why can't you use English? What century are you from?"

"The zeroth," replied Gabriel, as if the question were stupid.

Michael sighed. "Gabe, what's going on?" He glanced across the room to Emmaleigh, who had laid herself on her back and brought her hands to her head to stem the spinning. Michael wasn't sure whether she was even still awake.

"That pop you gave her? It was spiked. Didn't you know that?"

"No. Why would you make me give Emmaleigh a flew-- flewney-- flew--" He tripped over the word. "Why would you make me give her that?"

"In case the vodka wasn't strong enough."

"Vodka?" exclaimed Michael.

"Yeah. That drink was a vanilla vodka and Red Pop with a splash of cherry cough medicine and an 8- milligram flunitrazepam stinger. I invented it. I call

it a Permission Slip." Gabriel shrugged in false
modesty as if he were deserving of special recognition.
"I told you I'm more of a wingman angel. Not bad, huh?"
He winked to his own obscured reflection in a stainless
steel cabinet. Kody and Jordyn exchanged a glance,
their anxiety suddenly renewed.

"Jesus, Gabe..." said Michael over the radio.

"Don't blasphemy," Gabriel reprimanded. "So how much
did she drink?"

"The whole thing!"

"The whole thing? Holy shit. This should be a piece
of cake! You could lay an elephant with that." Gabriel
paused and digressed. "Not that you'd necessarily want
to. Leviticus 20:15 and everything." He shook his head.
"Such a waste of a perfectly good elephant."

"Gabe, what are you talking about?" Michael
demanded.

"What do you mean, 'what am I talking about?' You
don't get it?"

Michael didn't. "You mean you did this on purpose?"

"Of course," Gabriel responded.

"Why?"

"Am I really supposed to spell this out for you?
It's to loosen her up so you can sleep with her."

Michael wasn't sure he understood Gabe. It sounded
like he was telling him to penetrate her despite her
drunken, drugged stupor. But that couldn't possibly be
it, right?

Gabriel's voice crackled over the radio. "Was I too
subtle? I'm telling you to poke her."

"Gabe, I can't do that!"

"Sure you can! You're seventeen! You can probably do it twice."

"That's not-- I mean-- I thought--" Michael paced nervously in the classroom under the posters of ovaries and testes and the one misplaced poster about forms of compounding bank interest. "We're supposed to be the good guys!"

Gabriel sighed. "We _are_ the good guys! We're saving the world from Lucifer's reign of darkness!"

Michael scoffed. "By taking advantage of the most prudiest girl in the history of Crescent Lake High School?"

Gabriel admired his idealism and refuted with his own zeroth century pragmatism. "Sorry, Michael. But somebody's going to be 'taking advantage' tonight. That's just the way this has to be played out. I think we'd all prefer it be you."

There was a long pause. Michael said nothing, trying to gauge whether Gabriel's date-rape plan was an earnest one.

"Michael," Gabriel said, sensing his hesitation, "Lucifer wants the most virtuous girl in school."

"Yeah, so?"

Gabriel paused, surprised that he would need to be so explicit. "Take away her virtue."

There was a long, confused pause.

Kody and Jordyn traded a tacit look. Neither was comfortable with Gabriel's Plan A, but neither wanted to parent a demon, either.

Back in the Health/Home Ec classroom, Michael deliberated hard, looking over Emmaleigh in her vulnerable, unconscious stupor. He looked toward the ceiling for some reason as if divining some response from the universe. The radio crackled.

"I'm still here with your friends," Gabriel warned. "Jordyn, and literally half the rest of your school, are going to start birthing demons in mere hours. The world's going to end a few minutes after that. If you want to save your friends, yourself, all of humanity -- and even Emmaleigh herself -- you'll lay her."

Emmaleigh stirred a bit at the radio, woke slightly, and gave Michael a flirty, intoxicated smile.

"Oh, hey," she said to him. "Where'd you go?" Her solicitous eyes said the rest.

Michael glanced around the classroom; it was dark aside from the one fluorescent tube that was apparently un-turn-offable and ran 24 hours a day through nights & weekends & summers & Christmas & Columbus Day, which was recently re-named "Fall Break" on the district calendar.

A poster featuring a smiling teenage girl hung underneath the light. She seemed to glance back at him, a happy blonde girl sporting a hair style that went out when school yearbook portraits still had lasers in them, smiling and holding a basketball. Underneath read a mockingly prescient caption:

<u>Sex</u> <u>Can</u> <u>Wait</u>

Michael considered the advice. As he did, the radio crackled. "Just so we're clear," said Gabriel, "'Poke her' means have intercourse with her. Jam it in there. Get to slammin'." Michael blinked, preoccupied & overwhelmed, and clicked off the radio. He turned to

Emmaleigh, hoping she didn't hear the distant voice on the two-way.

"We're in trouble," he said to her. "We've got to stay as far away from everyone else as we can."

"Sounds like fun," she said.

No it didn't, thought Michael, as he escorted her out of the door. His destination was the safest place in the school that he could think of. That it had personal significance was merely coincidental.

"Michael...? Michael...?" Gabriel tried to reconnect with Michael over the two-way. It was fruitless. He dropped the radio to the table with resignation.

"Shit."

"What's the matter?" asked Kody. "He's got her, right? No matter what, we should be okay, right? You said it was prophesied."

"Yeah, but..." started Gabriel.

"Yeah but what?"

Gabriel frowned. "A prophesy itself doesn't guarantee something's actually going to happen."

Jordyn remembered something Gabriel said hours ago. "What did you mean before when you said, 'Now I get it'?"

He hesitated, reluctant to tell her. "Basically, sometimes the forces of good and evil place high stakes bets on people." He sighed. "Don't think of it as a prophesy. Think of it as a wager."

"What do you mean?" asked Kody. He didn't like the cryptic tone.

"This could still go wrong," said Jordyn.

Gabriel nodded. "Right."

Kody looked back and forth between Jordyn and Gabriel, his face sunken. "I've got to go find him!" he declared.

The prescribed ninth grade curriculum at C.L.H.S. made requisite reading of Chaucer, Hawthorne, and Shakespeare, who authored in languages that looked like English but read like gibberish:

"'Tis in vain to seek him here that means not to be found," they all once struggled through.

Kody didn't know what that meant in the 9th grade and didn't know it now. He departed the room, on a mission to find and assist his friend who might still ruin Homecoming. Gabriel didn't tell him he was being foolish and pointlessly impetuous. The die was cast.

Jordyn looked to Gabriel as if registering a silent, worrisome appeal. The angel shrugged. It was beyond them now. The ball was already in the air. Michael would either catch it or drop it.

Kody turned through the school systematically but with little luck. Most of the classrooms were locked, and the ones that were unsecured were either empty or occupied by couples who were not Michael & Emmaleigh. Twice Kody walked in on classmates who had attempted to indulge an INSATIABLE urge within them.

"I'm sorry," he'd say to both of them.

Undeterred, he continued turning out the school, taking caution when he returned to the fieldhouse to avoid crossing paths with Cayden, whom he now knew to be his best friend's mortal adversary. Fortunately, Cayden was nowhere among them, his location undisclosed somehow. Also missing was Michael's cheerleader date, Lucy. Kody didn't fixate on it. He was searching for Michael, not anyone else, though what advice or assistance he would provide upon discovering him, he still hadn't figured out.

He grew further deterred as the night wound on. As he accidentally encountered more of his classmates knowing each other in the biblical way. As he searched through the kitchen only to discover Caemron and some thin, beguiled freshman celebrating Lucky Tray Day, whereupon he pledged to bring his own sack lunch for the rest of the year. In the library, where he encountered a surprising number of grasshoppers. In the training facility, where he encountered even more.

By his third round through the school, Kody collapsed to the floor in sleepless fatigue and resignation. He nodded off for a moment, pledging to rest for a only a few minutes before renewing his vigilant search.

Far above the school, the distant stars spiraled in the night sky above as the hours dragged on.

THIS PAGE INTENTIONALLY LEFT BLANK

                                        Dear Emmaleigh,

    Hours had passed since Michael had absconded with

Emmaleigh and made a fortress of the chemistry

classroom, the very same one in which a benevolent

Creator had seated them together at the beginning of

the semester. The providence of the location had

nothing to do with his selection of it as a hideout.

Rather, it was the best defensive position he could

come up with: there were extra locks on the doors that

were intended to prevent some of the more

entrepreneurial students from requisitioning lab

equipment for private enterprise. Plus, were any of his

biblical adversaries able to breach them, the room was

stocked with nitric and hydrochloric acid, which

Michael had transferred to a series of spray bottles

that he wore on each hip like a Western hero

anticipating high noon. If Lucifer found his way in,

Michael would greet him with a 15.8 molar solution of burning agony and send him back to Hell without a face.

He rubbed his tired eyes and checked the clock above the blackboard, which now read only 06:42 despite his best efforts to advance it. It had a continually sweeping second hand that he had often telekinetically resisted. Chemistry was the only class in which he had hoped time would move slower, since it was the only class in which he was seated next to the most important girl to ever matriculate into Crescent Lake and his life. Tonight, however, he wished the clock would speed up. His adrenaline had kept him awake up until this point. That and his hunger pangs; everyone else had big meals in fancy restaurants, but Michael had eaten Pop Tarts for dinner for some reason. Not quite Pop Tarts, even. They were store-brand, the taste & consistency & nutritional value of corrugated cardboard. He did the math too slowly. Seventeen plus twenty-seven meant there were 44 minutes left. It felt like 44 hours.

His stomach growled. Emmaleigh slumbered through it in her drunkenness. She was blanketed in what was left of Michael's suit jacket.

He crouched above her and tried very gently to stroke her hair. It wasn't gentle enough; she stirred.

"Michael, what are we doing? Did I fall asleep?" she asked.

"Sort of," he guiltily replied.

She looked blankly around the room, trying to trigger memories of the last few hours. "Did we hook up?"

"No," he said, unsure whether she'd be disappointed or relieved.

She paused and smiled before reaching for his hand. "Do you want to?"

Michael felt his heart stop. "Emmaleigh," he said to her sweetly, "I can't tell you how badly I want that. But you're not feeling okay and it wouldn't be right considering, uh..." he searched for the right phrase. "Considering the situation." He felt proud of himself for demonstrating a chivalry he'd never before had an opportunity to display. "I promise to be right here for you now and until morning, but it won't be until tomorrow that we can start this relationship in the sort of way that would do right by you."

It was indeed a very touching tableau until she jolted up and barfed all over him.

Michael winced, covered in an artificially red-colored syrup that smelled both stale and fermented. "We'll probably leave that part out when we tell it to our grandkids."

Emmaleigh was still too drunk to summon the courtesy of an apology. She grabbed her temple and attempted to stand. "My head hurts," she said, falling back over. She tried again. "I have Advil in my locker. I'll be right back." But she fell again, immediately, like a newborn foal. She laughed until she winced from her headache.

"No!" Michael interjected, knowing Lucifer was probably somewhere lurking around the school, hoping to intercept her and bang her, etc. It was an unattractive

prospect for several reasons. He preferred to keep her
hidden.

"Er, I mean, let me go get it. You should just stay
off your feet and rest. What's your locker com?"

She smiled. It was sleepy and drunk but sincere.
"You really are a good guy."

Michael smiled back. He felt proud of himself. But

16:18 Pride comes before destruction.

One might have guessed he knew that, but he didn't.

It took several running attempts, but Emmaleigh
finally remembered the three digits of her locker
combination, and Michael left on the errand, poking his
head out the door and looking several times before he
was persuaded that there was no imminent danger. She
would be okay in his absence. He'd only be gone a
minute, and besides, he would use his swiped janitorial
key to lock the door behind him.

He went briskly down the halls until he arrived at
her locker. He was familiar with it. Could find it
blindfolded. Only a day ago had been thrown into it. He
swiftly twisted the dial and gained access.

Its tidiness did not make its innumerable contents
less intimidating. He rifled through the top shelf,
looking for the little plastic pill bottle. In his
haste he dropped a few random items: hair ties, a cup
of jelly pens and highlighters, a few desultory sheets
of paper. Eventually he encountered a bottle of skin
moisturizer. Though he was sensitive to her privacy, he
stole a moment to twist the cap and take a whiff from

the bottle, melting a little bit. He soon replaced the cap and returned it before locating the 24-count container of Advil. He stowed the bottle in his pocket and turned to quickly pick up his mess. And that's when he finally caught a glimpse of the newspaper clippings of Cayden McCaffrey, the ones that described his heroic exploits, taped inside the locker door. A black & white photo on newsprint of his 33-yard, last-second pass to defeat Meridian on opening weekend was center among them.

This didn't make very much sense. Michael investigated them. Maybe they were from the school paper? Perhaps among Emmaleigh's extracurricular activities, she served as layout editor, and there was something technical about these particular specimens that had made them display-worthy? No, that couldn't be it, he surmised; the newsprint and ink were too professional. They were from the sports section of the "real" paper, the one acquired on a street corner box or at the end of a driveway. He shook his head at them, choosing to dismiss the clippings as a peculiar aberration.

But his next discovery was much harder to disregard.

He bent to retrieve the items he had dropped on the floor in his haste. Among the loose papers that had fallen was a wide-ruled notebook sheet written entirely in his handwriting.

"Dear Emmaleigh..." it began. He froze.

It was the note he had written her, the embarrassing half-assed attempt at revealing his feelings. The one that had been surreptitiously stowed in the chemistry

notes he had lent to her. It had been segregated at the
top of her locker, which meant that it wasn't still
tucked within the lab notes, still waiting to be
discovered between tables of molar masses and atomic
weights. This could only mean that she had found it,
and if she found it, surely she too had read it. And
since she had denied ever encountering it, it could
only mean that she was quietly, politely, refusing its
sentiment.

Michael suddenly realized why she had been so eager
to tell him about her Homecoming plans on Friday
afternoon. She knew how he felt about her and wanted to
stave off the awkwardness of being asked out by him.

His crush was unrequited; his feelings for her
pitied.

The sting of the realization of this took the wind
out of him. He crumpled down to the floor under the
weight of the newsprint above him and remained there, a
million mile stare into space.

Dark Night of the Soul

He wasn't sure how long he had been sitting there on the floor beneath Emmaleigh's locker after his blindside collision. Maybe a minute, maybe five, maybe all night. Maybe the world had ended. How would he even notice? His had.

He walked slowly back to the classroom, each step demanding effort. When he turned the corner to the science wing hallway, he immediately noticed it: the light was on in their classroom-turned-hideout. It cast a bright rectangle on the commercial-grade carpet in the otherwise darkened hallway. The corridor was new enough that it still had that PVC smell to it.

He swallowed and closed the distance to the classroom. Entering, he saw Emmaleigh, still asleep where he had left her. But she had company.

"You didn't do it, did you?" asked Lucifer. He was asking whether Michael had laid her, though he already knew the answer. Michael said nothing, but his plaintive expression confirmed it. Lucifer smiled. "That's what she said about you. She said you're a good guy. She likes you. But not like that. She was too quick to let me know."

Lucifer spied the pathetic note in Michael's hand. "But you already found out about that, huh?" He sighed sympathetically. Michael still didn't say anything.

"Man, I'm sorry," Lucifer continued. "I feel for you. I really do. You pour your heart out to a girl and what does she do? She pretends to not even notice. Ouch."

"Maybe," said Michael, breaking his silence. "But she doesn't want you, either. She wants Cayden."

"Michael, to her, both he and I are the exact same person. In that capacity, I'm giving her exactly what she wants. It's actually what he wants, too. Check this out." He withdrew a small jewelry box from Cayden's suit jacket. Inside was a bracelet with small, unimpressive cubic zirconiums.

"It's shitty. And I don't just mean for you. This is a hideous bracelet. But the sentiment behind it is real. Cayden and Emmaleigh are stupid for each other."

It was strange to hear "Cayden" speak his own name in the third person.

Michael shook his head. "It doesn't matter. She's drugged. You'd be taking advantage, and Gabe said you can only take from someone who voluntarily gives."

Lucifer smiled. "Oh, but she did. She voluntarily allowed me to put that ring on her, and she voluntarily allowed herself to trust you." Michael shifted. A tell, maybe. Lucifer didn't notice.

"And what did you do with that trust?" he continued, unable to conceal the condescension, "You drugged her. Even if her trust were misplaced, she's still responsible for her own actions. Not me. In fact, I owe you some thanks. I was working every angle to get in there... but then you came in, and, well..."

Michael frowned.

"Don't worry about it. It's not your fault. Gabriel is an ass. You'd eventually realize that about him." He paused. "You know why?"

Michael shook his head, his skepticism increasingly endangered.

"Because he's on the wrong side."

Michael wasn't sure what this meant.

"I'm not a bad guy," Lucifer said. "I just want to have a good time like anybody else. The kind of time you should be having right now. You're young. You're healthy. You're not hideous looking."

Michael smiled at the very qualified endorsement. "That's, uh, thanks. That's kind of you. You should write greeting cards."

"The point is, you've got all you need in the world, but you're moping over a girl who doesn't truly care about you one way or another. Is that really worth your time?"

The point landed. Michael looked down at Emmaleigh, still sleeping. He shifted.

"Well, that's not totally true. She was a little bit jealous of all those other girls you very ungratefully exploded." Lucifer sighed, taking a moment to be annoyed at the slaying of two of his more faithful minions, before continuing. "But that's only because she likes the attention you give her. Funny, huh? She doesn't want you, but she wants you to want her. Oh well. Can't really blame her. She's seventeen. She's allowed to be capricious."

Michael looked at Emmaleigh again, as he had a thousand times before. But this time he appraised her as an adversary.

"I know. You're thinking, 'Why should I listen to him?' Right? 'He's evil.'" Indeed, this was what Michael was thinking.

"I bet Gabriel told you about my thousand years of darkness. More like a thousand years of awesomeness. Sixty second keg stands! Panties hanging from the ceiling fans! No hangovers! But you'll just have to take my word at that. I can tell you this, however. Tomorrow's going to be a brand new day. Where do you want to be when it happens? Enjoying it? Or moping over the loss of a girl you invented?"

Michael rubbed his eyes.

"It's not a rhetorical question. Quid pro quo, Michael: you let me leave right now with Emmaleigh, and I'll help you forget all about her by dawn."

"Why should I?" Michael asked. The question was firm but also solicitous. He wanted to be convinced.

"One? Because you want to forget about her. Obviously. Two, because you want to prove that if she doesn't have feelings for you, then neither do you for her. But most of all," Lucifer said, "because it's not fair to make you pretend to be a hero and suffer your own sword when the heroines choose the villains anyway."

There was a pause. Michael's apprehension was turning to acceptance. He shifted twice as he looked over Emmaleigh one more time. The girl who called him a good guy. The girl with someone else's pictures taped inside her locker. The girl who pocket-vetoed the brave, written declaration of his feelings for her.

He relented. "I'll forget all about her by dawn?"

Lucifer nodded. Michael ran his hand through his hair, the part he had drawn in his bedroom mirror hours ago now fully reversed. He was his own reflection of himself. A backwards version from an adjacent plane. Maybe this was who he always was.

He quashed only a fleeting ember of deliberation before officially surrendering.

"Okay," he agreed.

Lucifer lifted Emmaleigh in his arms like a bridegroom on the threshold of their new home and confidently carried her away to find a romantic place to consummate.

Michael, his hand still clutching his sad letter, the one that professed profound love for someone who found it a mere inconvenience, didn't even watch them go.

Michael had turned out the classroom light, preferring to wallow uninterrupted in quiet darkness. It was silent and cold and felt like a mausoleum, like something had recently died and been interred there.

He sat at his regular seat in the classroom, his chin resting in his hand, gazing into the infinite dark sky beyond the window. He wasn't looking at anything in particular. His stare was boundless, looking into the past and future, calculating how long it might take him to bridge the gap from one to the other. The clock on the wall no longer affected him. It may as well have stopped or run backwards or evaporated into the air.

He wasn't alone for very long. The cold silence was interrupted by the sound of heels slowly advancing. He turned toward them, bizarrely unalarmed. He was somehow at this moment incapable of alarm. Lucy stood in the doorway, her beauty intimidating.

"Hi, Michael," she said with passable empathy. "Are you okay?"

Michael didn't respond. His expression betrayed nothing; it was unclear whether he even heard the

question. Lucy stepped into the room, her heels echoing
with each careful step. Under a different circumstance,
the clicks of those heels against the tiled floor might
have been alluring.

"Is there anything that I can do for you?"

He remained silent, neither ignoring nor addressing
her, still staring into nowhere in particular. She took
two more slow steps across the hard surface of the
floor. Each step continued to click under each heel.

"This can still be a fun night, you know." Michael
indicated neither disagreement nor accord.

"You know, Michael, I'm not as bad as you think I
am," she said, advancing two more measured steps.

"And for you, I could be very, very good." Finally
there were no more clicks, no more echoes. She had
closed the distance between them. Standing above him,
she ran her hand through his hair. Far from recoiling
from her touch, he made eye contact with her and held
it.

"So what do you think?" she asked, raising her leg
several inches in order to reach and unbuckle her shoe.
It fell to the floor, one item down. "Want to have fun
with me?" she asked, reaching and removing the other
shoe. This one she dropped theatrically by her side.

He didn't respond, nor react. She smiled disarmingly
at him.

"Face it, Michael. We were fated to be together."
She lifted her dress ever so slightly in order to catch
enough slack to straddle him in his chair.

"So I've learned," he finally said with some degree
of acceptance. She guided his hands around her waist.

She held his gaze for a moment until something registered. She smiled wide.

"Not so shy anymore, are you?"

He smiled gently and without shame, somewhat ironically.

"I know you're kind of reserved around girls," she said, putting it generously. "But I know I can help you with that."

"Can you?" he asked. He said it like a challenge or an invitation. He wasn't teasing like before when he suggested they copulate while videotaping it, only to deliberately renege and flee through a structural vulnerability.

"Absolutely," she replied. "But only if you can help me with a little problem I'm having."

He watched himself as he ran two fingers along her side, up her waist, exploring the boundaries of both her curves and his own fleeting insecurities. "What's the problem?" he asked, anticipating the answer.

She was quiet, almost inaudible. She leaned in to his ear. "I need you so badly," she pleaded. "Do you think you can help me find God?"

For the first time in his long, sad, criminally uneventful history with the other sex, he didn't answer verbally. He ran his hand up her side, without direction, to her neck, which he pulled toward him, kissing her hard along her soft skin just underneath her perfect jawline. His right hand ran along her thigh and under her dress.

She moaned slightly while he kissed her neck.

"Is that good?" he asked.

"A little bit softer," she said. He did as he was told. She reacted in a way that suggested it was working.

She was a proving grounds, a testing site for experimental vehicles, and Michael decided he had something to test and something to prove.

She stole a moment to reach behind herself and unzip her dress. He helped her loosen it. But it was she who hesitated first.

"Shhhh," she said, standing over him. She rose and turned gracefully on her toes, a coquettish half-pirouette. Her thumbs traced the curve of her dress over her hips and plumbed their way under the hem. Underneath her gown, she slowly pressed her red lace panties down to the floor.

After two more steps, she was out of them. She teasingly bent to pick them up, then offered them to Michael. He didn't immediately accept, so she stretched them over his head, compelling him to wear them like a paper burger-stand hat. But he smiled. This was very much unlike him.

She sat on him once more. "What do you want to do?" she asked, knowing the answer. She unhooked the unfashionable bungee cord that had replaced his belt so many hours ago and unfastened the button of his pants without ever breaking eye contact.

He returned it, looking deeply into her eyes. She smiled at his tacit response.

"Lucy," he started.

"Yes?" she replied, forcing her chest into his face.
He stole two symmetrical kisses from either side of her
before looking up at her once more.

"There's something I need to tell you," he
continued, still kissing her with a confidence that
belied his limited experience there.

"Yes, lover?" she said, eyes closed, neck extended,
caught in the rhapsody of the moment.

He ran his hands through her hair and drew her close
to him, kissing her firmly on the mouth before pulling
her away. He smiled softly & confidently and said the
phrase.

"Deprendo qui Taco Bell calidum condimentum est
magis calidum quam Taco Bell ignis condimentum."

He was perfect at saying the wrong thing.

So perfect at it.

Lucy, the unholy demon ghoul, frowned as the words
came out and, in great ignominy to the kingdom of
darkness and its promised thousand years of
awesomeness, keg stands, and ceiling panties, exploded
into a cloud of locusts & legendary triumphant
righteousness, the kind that evades canonization but
still nestles its way into the Apocrypha, denied by
Protestants but unexpunged just in case.

Michael removed the feminine undergarment from his
head, used it to shoo the bugs away, and rose from the
chair with a temporary limp.

He re-fastened his makeshift bungee-cord belt and
re-buttoned his vomit-stained shirt.

31. Two lines are shown below in standard form. What is the *x*-coordinate of the point in the standard (x,y) coordinate plane at which these lines intersect?

$$6x - 2y = 14$$
$$15x - 5y = 20$$

A. 2
B. 3
C. 6
D. 15
E. These lines do not intersect.

Kody continued his desperate search for his friend, tracking through the hallways, when he heard it. Michael's voice. A loud, aggressive moan, an "ohhhhhhh!" that could have been an electrocution or a simultaneous ACL/MCL tear or, worse, the unmistakable sound of unmuted, unashamed orgasmic release. Kody sprinted in the direction of the sound.

Rounding the corner and turning into the chemistry classroom, he found Michael, his shoulders tensed, completely clothed, standing underneath the emergency chemical shower. It was a cold, industrial washplace consisting of a tall, bare pipe with a wide-diameter showerhead pointed directly down and a chain attached to a plastic handle that opened the valve. The water wasn't even heated. It wasn't designed for comfort. It was designed to aid those who were suffering from chemical burns. Or apparently much worse.

The freezing water sliced through him like a November downpour and clung to what still remained of his dress attire.

"What are you doing?" asked Kody.

Michael closed the valve and stood, shivering, on the tile. He didn't seem surprised or moved or relieved to see his friend. "I'm taking the coldest shower of my life," he said matter-of-factly.

Kody was both confused and alarmed. His questions came too fast. "What? Why? Where's Emmaleigh?"

"I don't know. Someplace." Michael was cavalier, too cavalier, despite shivering from the cold shower. He walked across the room, rifled through a drawer, and withdrew a laboratory fire striker.

"What do you mean?" implored Kody. "You lost her?"

Michael demurred, staring into space again. "I wish. Turns out I never had her to begin with." He snapped from the brief trance and swiftly placed a Bunsen burner, opened the valve, and ignited the gas. Kody watched Michael with perverse curiosity as he took a sheet of wide-ruled paper and fed it into the fire, where it quickly caught flame. Several of the pieces near where it had been ripped from the wire spiral of the notebook broke off and floated up with the heat, tired, eviscerated dreams being put out of their misery. He did this with the efficiency and indifference of a salary employee packing up a desk on Friday at 4:58p.

"Michael, what are you doing?" asked Kody with increasing concern.

He didn't answer. He simply flung the paper into a lab sink where it would harmlessly burn to reduced pieces of ash. He then warmed his hands over the Bunsen burner like some odd teenage hobo.

"Michael...?" he asked again.

Michael looked at his friend with encumbrance and decided to confess to his grade-school attempt to win Emmaleigh. He closed the valve on the burner and turned to Kody, hesitating slightly in embarrassment and shame. "Two weeks ago I wrote Emmaleigh a note telling her how great I thought she was." Kody didn't react, but Michael didn't give him a chance to react, preempting him. "I know. Pathetic. Save it. That's why I never told you about it."

Kody didn't care about this melodrama. So much more was at stake than his crush. "What are you talking about?"

"I hid it in some chem notes that she borrowed. When I asked her if she came across it, she said that she hadn't. But she did."

"Michael, who cares?" asked Kody. There was so so so much more at stake than this.

"You know what the really funny part is?" He dragged out the "really" to indicate that he didn't find any of this funny. "The really funny part is that she's got some huge crush on Cayden. And he's got some crush on her. It's no accident they're together. It's not 'fate'."

"I don't care!" Kody snapped, his frustration and panic boiling over. "Are you telling me she's missing?"

"No, I know where she is."

Kody breathed a sigh of relief. "Where?"

"She's with Cayden."

"What?" Kody cried, apoplectic. "How could you let that happen?" Michael picked up his jacket from the floor where Emmaleigh had used it as improvised bedding and started walking toward the door. He started to put the jacket back on, but noticed, entirely accidentally, that it still smelled like her. He frowned, stung again, and decided to just shed the damn thing. He stuffed it in the nearest trash can.

Kody repeated his question. "Michael, how could you let this happen?"

"What's the big deal?" Michael replied, walking again for the exit. "It's what she wants, right? Who am I to stop it?"

"You selfish asshole! Forget about your stupid fantasy girlfriend for ten seconds! Did you forget what's going on tonight?"

He reached the door and turned back to his friend. "No, I'm aware," he said, burdened.

"Then what about everyone else? What about the demons? The war? The inflation?" He pleaded. "Michael, what about Jordyn?"

Michael brought both of his hands to his head and scratched thoroughly, deeply, angrily, like a dog on its hind leg, as if he could literally shake his exhaustion or fatigue or burden. As he finished, he dragged his hands down over his face, temporarily drooping his eyelids to a surrealist extent. When he finally dropped his hands and looked back at Kody, he had a look of reassurance. A temporary composure. "Relax. She's going to be fine." He reached into his pocket and tossed something to Kody. It was a class ring. Lucifer's class ring. Emmaleigh's would-be wedding band.

"She broke their engagement." Michael shrugged, adding, "It happened before I poisoned her. Can't have an apocalypse without that," Michael announced.

Kody looked at him with relief. Even admiration. Michael gestured for it back; Kody obliged and returned it to him.

"I'm going home," Michael finally announced. "I'll call you tomorrow when I realize that this has all been a ridiculous dream." Michael turned out into the hallway, but Kody pursued him.

"Just so I'm sure," Kody asked, seeking complete, total reassurance, "That's that?"

"I don't see why not," replied Michael, continuing down the hall.

"So Cayden's with Emmaleigh, and they're probably going to..." he paused, unable to come up with a euphemism for sex that wouldn't injure his friend more than he'd already been injured. "Sorry." He bounded to keep up with Michael's pace.

"It's what she wants," Michael said bitterly, even though he knew the statement to be at least somewhat false. He continued treading down the hallway nonetheless, quickly approaching the first available exit.

They passed underneath the same blazing red digital clock that Emmaleigh had referenced only a day ago. It read 07:01. Michael held onto it a moment too long. There were 26 minutes left.

"But it's okay if they do," Kody paused again, grasping for benign words, "Er, do it... because you've got that ring?"

"Mm-hmm. And by the time it happens and he realizes he's been duped, it'll be too late. I'll be long gone."

Michael finally reached the end of the hallway. Installed there was a set of double-doors that led outside the school. It was a lonely and peculiar egress, one that exited to a somewhat wooded parcel rather than a parking lot or an atrium or a courtyard or something either conventional or useful. Furthermore, this set of double-doors, seldom used, sealed in an uncomfortable abundance of heat from the simmering baseboard heater enclosed within. It was at least 10 degrees warmer in there than it was in the remainder of the building. Some students had nicknamed it The Sauna for precisely this reason. But 119,000 square feet is difficult to HVAC homogeneously.

Michael pressed against the first set of doors, looking uneasy, the whole world still atop him.

Kody could tell Michael was unwell. "What's wrong?" he asked, not understanding his disposition. "You basically saved the world! You're a hero!"

Michael ignored him, trying with effort to evade both Kody's dubious accolades and some growing burden within him. But as soon as he laid his hands on the bar of the second set, he abruptly stopped, arrested by some malignant cause of distress. He stood there for a moment, frozen, unable to move. Kody looked on in anxious concern.

Finally, Michael mused something under his breath to himself.

Kody didn't make out what he said. He asked him to repeat it. Michael didn't oblige; he was still thinking too hard to himself. He looked up, his hands on the bar, poised and ready to press forward and release himself from the ordeal, leaving the school and its fate behind him. He noticed the stenciled letters that were written, from his vantage, in reverse: "Doors are to remain locked during school hours." These doors were always locked. He had never, in three years on campus, seen anyone enter or exit through them.

Somehow this triggered him to consider something else with increased profundity. A moment passed before Kody called to him again.

"Michael, did you hear what I said? You're a hero."

Michael turned. He did not feel heroic. "Yeah, got it. Hero," he said, unimpressed with himself. He looked to his friend. "You know what the last thing Emmaleigh said to me was?"

Kody shook his head.

"The last thing she said to me before I let him carry her off was 'You really are a good guy.' She might like Cayden more than me, but she's not ready to give it up to him, and it wasn't right of me to surrender her to him."

Kody shrugged. "So...?"

"So I'm going to go stop him."

This didn't totally register with Kody. Michael's
plan already seemed to make sense. Why jeopardize it?

Nevertheless, Michael turned around, back into the
foyer of the peculiar, misplaced exitway, and gave Kody
one final instruction. "Bring this to Gabe. Guard it
with your life." He handed the cursed class ring to
Kody, who accepted it and nodded, still unpersuaded of
the viability of this new plan. But his dissent was
immaterial. Michael resolutely strode down the hall, a
man on a mission. Purpose for the first time.

Michael marched the hallway, retracing the path that was mere moments ago his cowardly escape. Back past the glowing red digital clock that now read 07:04. Past the chemistry classroom where he had sheltered Emmaleigh from danger before shamefully becoming complicit in that very same danger. Past the dark classrooms that were empty but still warm from the discreet assignations that had occurred in them over the course of the night. Back through the long hallway that as recently as Friday at dismissal he had swam against.

This time he moved swiftly.

He passed through the domed atrium where the four major wings of classroom space intersected, hardly pausing to look up through the enormous panes and confirm the imminently fleeting darkness above. He checked Kody's watch, not for the current time, of which he was acutely aware, but for what it represented.

He passed through a long corridor connecting the academic wings to the athletic & musical & administrative & utility wings. Hung on the wall along this long, airport-terminal-ish hallway were the complete class photos of every graduating class in the history of the district, all the way back to the school consolidation in 1922. Their hair styles and attire changed. Somehow their smiles didn't. If Michael had stopped to look, he might have found his adversary in each one of them. He was there, omnipresent, smiling back in all of them. Every Goddamn one.

Before he reached the end of the corridor where it terminated into the commons, he detoured into an administrative hallway. Hours ago he had been in here to seize the public address microphone. Now he tested the door to the athletic director's office and found it fortuitously unlocked. The AD was known to keep a baseball bat behind his desk, something that tied him to the glory days of his one semi-pro single-A season. He had well-known habit of carrying the bat around like a security blanket, something for which the faculty and student body alike gave him good-humored ribbing. It helped him think, the genial AD would rebut.

Michael gave himself permission to borrow it. He had a similar use in mind.

He exited the AD's office but was distracted by the smell of cigarette smoke wafting through the back hallway. Michael, curious, followed the smell down the passage, which ran in the opposite direction from which he had entered. He traced it until the narrow hallway terminated in the main office, where the secretaries sat daily, like air traffic controllers, pursuing truancies and lining up the ill and injured for early parental pick-ups. There were two couches in the waiting area. One of them was occupied.

"Hi guys," said Michael to the pair. It was Goth Dillon and his junior date. "Goth" wasn't his Christian name, of course, merely a salutation that had been bestowed upon him by the remainder of the senior class. To his credit, Goth Dillon was too practiced at nihilism to mind. They both wore ironic dress attire; rather, when they had arrived at the dance, they wore ironic dress attire. At this particular moment, they wore a deliberate quantity of eyeliner and little else.

"We thought the door was locked," said Dillon, apologizing for himself while wrapping himself in a burgundy leisure jacket. Michael shrugged. Dillon's date, covering herself, looked at the baseball bat apprehensively.

Dillon had been smoking since the 8th grade, but this was his first cigarette in this particular clichéd situation. Michael gestured to Dillon's cigarette. "Do you mind?" he asked.

In another minute, Michael had re-entered the commons area where mere hours ago he had sauntered in in a jacket, tie, and clean shirt. He possessed none of those things now. The fieldhouse was adjacent, and the students there were still rapt by the impromptu all-nighter, a Church of Satan lock-in. He arrived at the final stop before his ultimate destination: the trophy case that housed so many accolades & memorabilia & nostalgia. One item in particular struck his interest, a class ring from 1984. It was simultaneously unremarkable and anachronistic. In its new home, it looked like a museum piece. If any of the freshmen or sophomores took thirty seconds to consider its existence, they would have dismissed it as an inconsequential antiquity. The school building from which the Class of '84 had graduated was now a middle school. The Class of '54 had graduated from a building that was now a community center. The Class of '24 graduated from a building that had long since been razed and turned into a children's park with equipment the school board had recently contracted for removal due to the obscene insurance premiums associated with them. Time and tide etc.

He paused before the glass trophy case and determined a graceless snatch-and-grab would be perfectly sufficient. After all, not only was the entire world at stake, but he hadn't seen a chaperone in hours. Not since he exploded the last one after being confronted by her generous bare bosom.

He lifted the baseball bat and went yard against the trophy case, cracking it first into a shattered spider web and then, with two more swings, reducing the pane to felled shards of jagged glass. He discarded the bat on the bed of debris like he just hit a walk-off ninth-inning RBI in May.

He efficiently seized the class ring, the object
that drove him to misdemeanor vandalism, and gave it a
cursory inspection. He fitted it to his right pinky
finger as if he had made himself a mob boss. While
appraising its value as a decoy and determining it was
adequate, he was again interrupted by a voice behind
him.

"Hey, there you are!"

Michael had lost count of how many times he had
heard this dreadful phrase. He turned toward the
source, expecting to find a beautiful girl bent on
destroying him and was not disappointed. This time it
was Katie Van Pelt, the Homecoming Queen. She still
wore the tiara she had won at halftime the previous
evening. Michael knew her only vaguely, from maybe a
few classes they had shared over the last three years.
But she ran outside his limited social circle. Michael
really knew only two things about her: first, the
knock-off Swarovski in the tiara really complemented
her eyes. Second, he wouldn't hesitate to transform her
into a Plague of Egypt.

"I've been looking for you. I was kind of hoping
that maybe we could, you know, talk? Or like, hang
out?" she said with borrowed confidence.

"You too?" he asked her.

"What do you mean?"

He paused, circumspect of her motives. She looked
down at the floor and brushed her hair back in a
nervous way that was supposed to invite conversation.
It appeared she was about to say something, but every
time she attempted to speak, she hesitated, rejecting

every word and phrase that was fruitlessly nominated
for the task.

Michael hardly noticed these things. He was
preoccupied with trying to determine whether Katie, the
duly-elected and faithfully-serving Homecoming Queen,
had always been a treacherous demon from Hell. He
braced for the anticipated result and tested the
hypothesis:

"Possum invitare amicus?"

But nothing happened. She just stood there,
confused. She didn't speak Italian. It wasn't even an
offered course at Crescent Lake.

"What?" she finally asked.

Michael was somehow more unsettled than he was
relieved at her failure to explode. "Huh," he muttered
to himself.

"Listen, Michael--"

He interrupted her. "I'm really sorry, but I'm late
for something. I've got to go."

"Where do you have to go?" she asked. It sounded
distinctly like a brush-off.

"The pool." There was a strange pause, before he
realized that he had revealed too much. "I've got to
put in some laps," he elaborated. The burning cigarette
in his lips did not help corroborate his aerobic
intentions.

"Oh," she said flatly, confused & visibly hurt.

He sized up Katie one more time, trying to figure
her out. This encounter made no sense. He slowly backed
away with vigilant caution, as if he were confronted
with a junkyard dog or a bear or a hippopotamus with a

junkyard dog on its back. She watched him go with an
emotion that Michael was legendarily unequipped to
recognize. Determining, however, that he was out of
imminent danger, Michael turned and strode down the
hallway with his prize class ring, leaving the
Homecoming Queen eerily deflated. He had only minutes
to get to the natatorium, and that's if he weren't
already too late.

He couldn't explain how he knew, but he knew that he
had taken her to the pool. Somehow he just felt it.
Knew it with one-hundred percent certainty. Maybe that
was the fate part that had earlier eluded him.

The natatorium was cool, quiet, and clean. The lights suspended from the ceiling were turned off, and the massive skylights still dark, but the underwater lights cast an ambient blue light through the surface of the water that danced on the walls and reflected throughout the room. One might have even called it a romantic location. It was certainly a secluded one.

Lucifer had built a bed of clean white pool towels on the deck, upon which he had laid Emmaleigh, still unconscious from all the liquor & cold medicine, fatigue & flunitrazepam. He shook her gently to try and wake her from her deep slumber. It would "count" no matter what, but he would've preferred she be present for it.

"Emmaleigh, my love," he said to her. "Wake up."

She remained passed out, however, and he shook her
again. "Emmaleigh...?"

She slowly stirred. "Michael?" she asked, eyes still
heavy and closed.

"It's me, Cayden."

"Cayden? Where are we?"

"We're all alone, dear," he said. "I can finally
give you that thing you wanted."

"What are you going to give me?"

Lucifer smiled. He couldn't help himself. "I'm going
to give you my staff, babe. I'm going to take you to
Heaven."

There was a long silent pause. It was unclear
whether she heard the innuendo or had simply fallen
back to sleep.

"I'm tired," she finally said, mumbling the words,
which were designed neither to indicate consent nor
register protest. She was merely still intoxicated. She
rolled to her side, her back facing him, and fell back
to sleep.

Lucifer evaluated the situation one more time before
deciding to give her the courtesy of sleeping through
it. He proceeded in a manner that was methodical but
not urgent, removing his own jacket first, followed by
his uneconomic, non-reversible black belt and button-up
Oxford shirt, which he cast aside, done with them
forever. He peeled off his A-shirt and folded it too by
his side. Then he turned to Emmaleigh, surgically
lifting her dress up along the thigh and tugging
somewhat disgracefully at her underwear. He scooted
along the floor while removing them, deciding to take

caution not to wake her. When he finally slipped the prize from her foot, he took a moment to savor the imminent victory.

They were white and some combination of natural & synthetic fibers, nothing particularly "sexy" or even remarkable about them save for how the fabric returned the light. Indeed, Lucifer was struck by it: the intensity of it seemed to increase, practically glow. This was peculiar, thought Lucifer, and he was right. He looked up to the ceiling.

Someone or something had ignited the heavy high bay lights suspended above. They were the type of enormous commercial bulbs that lit slowly, gradually, but eventually reached a blinding 13,000 lumens each. For now, they glowed dimly above, quietly humming like jet engines that had just been fired from a rest, and they painted the reflective whites in the room like road signs at night. Lucifer looked up toward them like they were witnesses that were stepping from the shadows.

"Hey Lucifer!" yelled the torch bearer who had lit them. "I hope you brought protection."

The Omnipotent Prince Angel of Darkness stood and turned toward the intruder. It was Michael, standing confidently in the tile natatorium entryway, an unkempt mess whose ordeal of a night was written all over him: his tie & jacket missing; shirt buttons held on by threads; tiny synthetic fibers from the school's drop-ceiling tiles littered his hair and collar; his pants, sans belt, fastened with a bungee cable. Above his lipstick stained collar were the combat bruises of Jessica's violent kisses. His hair was mussed and his eye blackened and he held his arm with a limp, having gashed and bruised it in his earlier fall from the auditorium catwalk to the stage. His shoes were missing. His right hand was dyed green, the tattle-taling of a fire alarm that had squealed on him as a criminal but failed to alert anyone to the crime. The crisp white of his shirt was stained with red number-5 colored vomit. It had a faint aroma of artificial vanilla.

Despite his attire, however, he looked different. He took a long, calm, cool, collected draw off of the cigarette he had copped off of Goth Dillon before choking on the smoke and coughing in a calm, cool, collected way.

"Michael?" interjected Lucifer. "Where's Lucy?"

"I exploded her," he said, flicking the cigarette into the pool. "That's right. I explode things now." He grinned as if he were bragging to a friend about the long list of girls he had conquered and added to his history. "I exploded all of them. I exploded all of them so hard."

Lucifer studied Michael's new, defiantly confident disposition. "I thought we had an arrangement...?"

"We did," Michael said, "but I changed my mind." He gestured toward Emmaleigh. "In fact, so did your girlfriend." He lifted his pinky finger, revealing the cursed class ring on the green digit. "Your ass got dumped."

Lucifer, in a rare moment of confusion and maybe even panic, glanced back to Emmaleigh's hand. Missing from her finger was the class ring. She was unwedded to him. How did he not notice?

"Whoops!" said Michael with mocking alarm. "So what do you say, Lucifer? Want to be bad?"

Lucifer stood, took a long breath, and advanced toward Michael in a smooth yet villainously creepy way. He practically floated. Michael gulped.

Gabriel sat in a padded green vinyl rolling chair at
his plain, undecorated steel desk. The seat was covered
in some places in duct tape; in other places, the tears
went unsutured. He rested his head in his hands and
watched the clock on the wall, the minute hand creeping
closer to the red line he had drawn there more than
twenty-four hours ago.

Jordyn was still with him, too tired to stay awake
but too anxious to fall asleep. She leafed through the
pages of some old yearbook stuffed with Gabriel's
foreign notes. The paper was thin and brittle like an
old phone book. She handled it delicately, as if it
contained some desperate clue to help stave off their
imminent fate, a fate to which Gabe, to her disdain,
had already resigned.

It was at this moment that the radio clicked back to life.

"Gabe, are you there?"

It was Kody. He had found Michael's abandoned two-way radio, Pheidippides broadcasting from Marathon.

Gabriel seized the radio. "Kody?"

"Yeah, it's me," he said. "It's over!" he announced in triumph. "I'm on my way back right now."

Jordyn sat up, trying to fight a cautious, premature smile of relief. Gabriel stood. "What do you mean?" he asked with urgency.

"I'm bringing back the class ring. The contract, remember?"

Gabriel considered this. "He's got her ring?"

"Michael said that Emmaleigh took it off or something. She was pissed at him and took it off. Then Michael stole it. Then he gave it to me. Michael says it's a voided contract, right?"

"Huh," grunted Gabriel, pacing again through the janitorial shop. Yeah, this could work. In retrospect, it even seemed like a cleaner solution than his original Plan A, if somewhat more legally ambiguous in the anti-climactic nuances of contract law.

"Put Michael on," Gabriel demanded.

"He's not here," Kody replied.

"Where is he?"

"Apparently when he got the class ring, he gave up Emmaleigh to Cayden. Cayden doesn't know he's been tricked."

Gabriel hesitated, less reassured than he was a moment ago.

Jordyn was struck by something else. "So Michael just left her to be date raped by Cayden?" she asked with scorn. Gabriel repeated the question into the radio, altering her statement for editorial tone.

"Well, that's the thing. He realized it wasn't fair what he did to her, so he went to stop them," Kody replied.

"Oh no." Gabriel frowned.

"Oh no, what?" asked Kody, suddenly alarmed that Gabriel did not share his sanguinity.

"Michael can't win a physical altercation against Lucifer! And even if he could, Lucifer is only borrowing Cayden's body. He can't injure "Lucifer" without injuring a completely innocent classmate."

"Oh," said Kody.

"And God forbid," continued Gabriel, "If Michael 'kills' Lucifer, he'll only really be killing Cayden!"

Kody scoffed at Gabriel's hypothetical concern. "That couldn't happen. Cayden's like 6'3", 210. If anyone's getting killed, it would be Michael."

This was followed by a sudden moment of panic as everyone simultaneously realized it: Michael was going to literally get himself killed.

"Oh shit! I've got to help him!" said Kody.

"No, stop! Wait!" yelled Gabriel into the radio. But it was too late. Kody had, in a renewed state of absent-minded panic, dropped the radio and sprinted off in the direction he had last seen Michael abscond.

Gabriel tried the radio again, but there was no response. Frustrated, he tossed it onto the floor, all his hard work, his planning, his careful pharmacology, suddenly in jeopardy.

"What's the matter?" asked Jordyn.

Gabriel glanced one last time at his clock. The minute hand at this moment crossed over the red line he had drawn on its face so many hours earlier. It was an astronomical gauge, a two-minute warning sort of thing. Rays of light birthed at that precise moment in the center of the solar system would, in 8½ minutes, arrive unimpeded.

The dawn was coming.

"Your boyfriend," Gabriel said, "who has Lucifer's class ring, is out there trying to find Michael, who himself is trying to find Lucifer. He's bringing the ring right back to him."

Gabriel dashed out of the room, himself on an almost-certainly futile mission to stop the guy who was trying to stop the other guy who was trying to stop the other guy.

For the first time all night, Jordyn realized that she had started to show. She threw up.

Baby Bye Bye Bye

In the celebrated fieldhouse, kids continued to party like it was 1999. The exhausted DJ checked his watch. It was finally nearing seven thirty.

"Thanks for being such a great crew tonight, Crescent Lake High School," he announced over the trail end of Sisqo's Thong Song. "Looks like this one is going to be the last one of the night." Synthesized strings ushered in the final dance of Homecoming at Crescent Lake High School.

The students continued dancing, oblivious to the cruel fact that all of the girls were imminently due to give birth to demon offspring who would burst forth from their vaginas to spread war & death & famine and enslave their fathers.

Lucifer advanced on Michael, trying to control his rising anger. "Give me back that ring, Michael," he said, closing in measured steps.

"Why don't you come get it?" Michael mocked, striking a kung-fu pose.

Lucifer closed the distance between them and, swatting Michael's hand away, threw him into the tile floor.

Michael wiped blood from his lip. "Give up yet?" he asked the sinister angel. Lucifer was undaunted. He stepped on his throat.

"Give me the ring."

"No!" said Michael. Lucifer applied more pressure.

"Give me the Goddamn ring, Michael!"

Michael tried to shake his head but he could hardly move under Cayden's impressive dress shoe. He could

hardly choke down a breath, either; he figured he might
only have a few seconds of consciousness left. His
peripheral vision started dimming to black.

Lucifer said it slowly. "Give... me... the ring."

"Go... to... Hell..." Michael managed to choke out
between furious, labored gasps for air, as he turned
deeper shades of blue.

"Hell is coming to us, Mike. Now give me that ring."
He applied all the pressure he had been holding back.
Michael's vision left him. "Give it."

Michael, summoning his last ounce of energy, offered
up the ring in his palm and, right before Lucifer could
clutch it away, chucked it in the pool.

"You dick!" cried Lucifer, still standing on
Michael's throat. He could invest a few more seconds
and finish the job, but he simply didn't have a few
seconds to spare. He released the pressure and rushed
to the pool, diving like an Olympian and leaving a
supine Michael crumpled on the tile. Michael rolled
into a fetal position, gasping huge breaths of air. His
vision gradually returned as he stumbled to his feet
and groped his way toward Emmaleigh. Lucifer,
meanwhile, was under the surface of the water,
searching for the ring.

"Emmaleigh! Emmaleigh, wake up!" Michael exclaimed
as he reached her, a sleeping beauty in a perfect
dress, spread gently over a sterile white pile of robes
& towels. He shook her by the shoulders. "Emmaleigh,
wake up! Please, wake up, Emmaleigh!" Her eyes slowly
opened, but too slowly & too groggily. Gabe's Red Pop
still maintained its hideously salutary effect.

Lucifer, meanwhile, swiftly surfaced from the pool and stroked his way efficiently to the tile. Having retrieved the ring, he climbed from the water and advanced toward both his bride and his nemesis, who was kneeled over her. "Emmaleigh! Wake up!" pleaded Michael as he jostled her by the shoulders. He noticed something on the pile of towels beside her, snatched it, and shook her again. "And for the love of God, put your underwear back on!" Lucifer, approaching from behind, grabbed Michael by his arm and flung him effortlessly into the pool.

Emmaleigh's eyes opened. "Cayden?" asked Emmaleigh, slowly waking. "What's happening?"

"Go back to sleep, my love," reassured Lucifer, slipping the ring back onto her finger. "Close your eyes. It's all okay."

Except it wasn't. As Lucifer groped again at Emmaleigh's dress, readying himself to mount her, this time with more urgency than romance, he heard a tiny metallic clang. The poorly-sized ring had slipped right off her finger, which meant only one thing -- the ring wasn't his. It was the ancient one lifted from the trophy case, the one Michael had freed with the AD's baseball bat.

"Oh, God damn it!" exclaimed Lucifer as he realized that he had now twice been duped by what he had originally calculated to be such an intractably unimpressive foe. He looked toward the skylight to check for indications of the imminent dawn. The blackness had turned gray, the stars above obscured and

muted by pre-dawn twilight. The inevitable sunrise was
only minutes away.

Michael had righted himself in the pool and was now
treading water, pleased with his latest ruse.
"Something wrong, buddy?" he called out.

Lucifer turned toward him, oddly calm. He had been
stymied so far but not yet bested. He stole a deep
breath and focused intently on the water. At that
moment, a button on Michael's shirt, the superfluous
one that fastens the collar to the shirt above the tie,
dislodged, floated away, and was promptly consumed by
the filter.

Lucifer closed his eyes, concentrating hard on
something. Michael was confused at his yoga-like Zen
until he felt the water temperature begin to rise.
Every single gallon of water in the NCAA standard-sized
pool began to simmer. Lucifer opened his eyes,
confirming his efforts. He was using some awful
telekinesis to raise the pool to a boil. Thin layers of
steam floated off the surface as if it were a massive
spa.

"Ow... ow... ow...!" Michael protested. This was a
dick move. "C'mon, you asshole!" But Lucifer didn't
relent. In fact, he dove into the pool, now 108°F and
climbing, and pursued Michael in swift freestyle
strokes.

"Shit! Shit shit shit!" Michael took fledgling
breaststrokes toward the opposite tiles, fleeing again
the Prince of Darkness. Michael reached the edge of the
pool just as the water reached an untenable temperature
& just as Lucifer caught up with him, scarcely escaping

his grasping hand. Michael ran toward the narrow,
winding staircase that ascended ever upward toward the
10-meter board. It was somehow the only acceptable
option in his increasingly incautious flight-over-fight
mind.

"I! Hate! High! School!" he exclaimed between
breaths as he ran up the twisting staircase.

Michael reached the top of the platform and
evaluated his options. There were now only two grim
paths back to the ground: a 10 meter, 33 foot leap to a
hard, cold tile floor or an equidistant plummet into 74
thousand cubic feet of viciously boiling water. Steam
poured off the surface and rose to the platform.
Michael took a deep breath of the air.

It was hot as hell.

Michael darted across the top of the platform,
considering these options. A single rope, the synthetic
kind that's used to separate pool lanes, hung in
suspension across the end of the diving dock as if to
prevent unsupervised diving. It supported a sign that
read "Closed". Michael didn't appreciate the irony.

He looked toward the ceiling: the skylights were
warmer, but the dawn wouldn't arrive quickly enough for
him to wait out the clock up there. "Shit, Michael!" he
said to himself, "Think! Think!" He looked down to
check on Emmaleigh, who was slowly returning to some
form of conscious lucidity. Satisfied she was out of
immediate danger, he attended again to his even more
immediate peril.

"C'mon, what would Jesus do?" he asked himself
aloud. Gabe's words echoed through his mind:

"Sure, every once in a while, he'll show up to give everyone fish..."

"Fish tacos!" Caemron added in his memory. Michael suddenly got the reference.

He considered what Churchy Girl, whose name he had again forgotten, might do:

"Want to stick your hand up there and find out?" she answered in his memory.

Michael paced harder and faster. "Quid derelquiste me?" asked Michael aloud. But no one responded.

He stopped, froze, and looked again at the rope with academic interest.

Meanwhile, Lucifer had pulled himself from the pool and reached the base of the winding stairs. He left a blazing trail of fire as he climbed each step in steady pursuit, his adversary surely trapped -- verily paralyzed -- atop the platform. Indeed, when he reached the summit, Lucifer saw his opponent crouched over the ledge of the deck.

"Give me the ring, Michael."

Michael stood and turned toward Lucifer, his back to the ledge, which was no longer protected by a single line of synthetic twine. "I don't have it. I hid it and you'll never find it. Not by dawn."

"Bullshit. I'd wager a thousand years that you gave it to your friend Kody. Where is he?"

Michael attempted a poker face, unwilling to say or do anything that would betray Kody's location. Unfortunately, Kody would betray himself; he was at the moment rushing through the hallway entrance to the natatorium, continuing his frantic search for Michael, hoping to intercept him before he would either kill Cayden or, more likely, be killed by Cayden.

And that's when, from the lonely entrance to the natatorium, Kody had finally found Michael. "Michael!" he called out. "Don't do it!" Kody was afraid that somehow, some way, Michael was winning the physical altercation and about to dispatch Lucifer, possessor of Cayden's body, and subsequently dispatch his classmate.

But that was not the situation.

"You've got to be kidding me," muttered Michael to himself, surprised at his ever-increasing bad luck. Lucifer, smiling, took a step toward Michael, perched over the edge of his own demise. He advanced with a fiendish design of flinging the seventeen-year-old into the boiling pool. With Michael cast to the lake of fire, Lucifer would then leap to the ground to recover the ring from Kody, re-wed Emmaleigh, and conquer the world by satisfying the one solitary feat demanded of him.

Michael slumped, resigning himself to his fate. At least so it seemed. Lucifer took Michael square by the shoulders and delivered his sad epitaph. "All this for a girl you'll never hook up with? Kind of pathetic, Mike."

Michael mustered a sad accord. "I know, right?"

Lucifer held him even tighter by the shoulders. "You know what happens next, don't you?"

Michael expelled a breath of air and looked up, directly in Cayden's eyes, and held his gaze. He nodded his head.

"Yeah, I know what happens next," Michael said. "Baptism." He smirked, exuding a peculiar confidence of one who was now falling back onto an extemporaneously plotted Plan C. Lucifer didn't have a chance to attempt to interpret his response.

Michael, summoning whatever strength he had left, grabbed Lucifer with both hands and threw all of his weight toward the pool. In an instant they were both free-falling toward the boiling abyss, Lucifer first but Michael right behind him, a mere 1.43 seconds from breaking the surface of the water and having the natatorium renamed the Michael Williams & Cayden McCaffrey Memorial Pool.

Lucifer's mind calculated faster than the time it took for them to fall, and in that instant he wondered if Michael was willing to kill himself in a suicide dive in order to thwart his plan and subsequently save Emmaleigh. The fire wouldn't kill Lucifer, of course, but it would destroy the body he had lawfully & contractually leased. The student body would mourn the congenial, admired captain of the football team. They wouldn't understand and therefore wouldn't mourn the guy who twice ruined Homecoming. There would be no hero's funeral for him. No twenty-one gun salute. No plaque or paver to record his Labours.

If that were true he had thrice underestimated Michael. They plummeted to the boiling inferno.

But then, mid-air, in a violent snap, they suddenly stopped plummeting.

They swayed for a moment in the wide arc of a pendulum before coming to a static dangle halfway between the 10 meter platform and the rolling surface of the pool. It took Lucifer a moment to realize what had transpired.

Michael's ankle was wrapped and bound with the 30-inch bungee that Gabriel had given him, the one that had served as his makeshift belt, and the bungee itself was tied in an impressive knot into the pool rope that had insufficiently performed its task of preventing unauthorized diving. The catch, which had spared both their lives, had nonetheless friction-burned his ankle and maybe even dislocated it.

Michael, however, didn't feel the intensity of the pain or the blood run from his broken skin because he had in a mere moment reversed the advantage that Lucifer held at the top of the platform. Tethered there by the rope, albeit precariously and painfully, Michael was protected from the fall, but Lucifer was suspended only by his tight grip on Michael's wrist, which Michael endeavored to shake, condemning him to the fiery, rolling boil. Lucifer struggled to keep the grip, re-evaluating his situation. They remained suspended in this fashion.

"Let me back up, Michael," demanded Lucifer, still cool but now willing to bargain once again.

"No!" Michael hollered back.

"Let me back up and I'll give you anything you want. Money?"

"No!" he reprised.

"Women?"

"Like Lucy? No thanks."

"That pirate themed Lego set you wanted for Christmas when you were nine but your parents said was too expensive?"

"They didn't say it was too expensive; they said I'd lose all the pieces, you idiot." Michael was unflappable, his blood coursing with biblical righteousness and teenage epinephrine.

Lucifer glanced to the skylight. There was no longer any use in bargaining; even the brightest stars had been erased, washed into a pre-dawn haze. He'd failed. He tried to conceal the disappointment that he had come so close and lost. His next opportunity wouldn't come

for 1000 years. But, he assured himself, it would come.
He relaxed his grip and gave up the struggle.

"This isn't over, Michael."

"Oh! What are you going to do? Drop me into a pool
of boiling fire? That'd be a neat trick, since I'm the
one who's about to do that to you right now!"

"You broke our arrangement. I'll be back for you,
you know."

"Yeah, back as soup," Michael mocked. "Apage
Santanas," he said with action movie precision as he
loosed his grip, remanding Lucifer back to the
lamentable depths of Hell.

But "Lucifer" didn't respond. Instead:

"Michael? What's going on?"

The disposition was totally different. The surprise
and confusion was genuine. This was not Lucifer.
Lucifer was gone. Disappeared. Vanished. Cayden -- the
real Cayden -- was all that remained in his place.
Michael realized this too late and could do nothing but
watch helplessly as Cayden fell the remaining 15 feet
into a calm, cool sea of sterile water.

Michael checked his watch. 7:27am. The skylights
above were bright with sunlight. The Homecoming Dance
was over.

00:00:00

Moments later Cayden was dragging himself from the pool while Emmaleigh grasped her head, wincing from a hangover she did not remember acquiring. Cayden looked around the room, utterly confused as to where he was or how he got there, like waking from a coma while in motion. He had once fallen asleep on a sunny afternoon during the first week of daylight standard time and awoken at 7:15, the room pitch black, thinking it was AM rather than PM and cursing that he was late for school and had slept in his clothes. He rushed downstairs under this impression until he was struck by the surreal scene of seeing his family seated leisurely at the dinner table around a half-consumed lasagna.

This was logarithmically worse.

Soaked through his clothes, he recognized Emmaleigh on the pool deck and approached her with a slew of

1

unanswerable questions. "Emmaleigh? What are we doing here? What's going on?"

At the sound of his voice, she recoiled and scrambled to her feet. "Stay away from me!" she yelled back at him.

"Emmaleigh, are you okay?"

"I said stay away from me, you asshole!"

Cayden froze before taking a cautious step back. "Emmaleigh, what are you talking about? What's the matter?"

"What am I talking about? I'm talking about what you were trying to do to me all night!" Her rising anger and blood pressure caused her already aching head to pound. She had slept off her stupor but not the aching pain it had invited. She crouched and put her hands on her temples. "Oh my God, what did you do to me?"

"What do you mean? I didn't do anything to you. I swear to God, I don't know what you're talking about! I don't even know where I am or how I got here!"

Michael, meanwhile, had untangled himself from the bungee, descended from the ten-meter platform, and crept slowly toward them on the deck. As the only witness among the three to not have been either drugged or possessed by a supernatural Bible creature, he was unsure to what degree he ought to weigh in with the peculiar, unadulterated truth.

"Don't talk to me like I'm stupid!" Emmaleigh cursed at Cayden. "We went to the auditorium together and then I don't know what you did to me because I don't remember anything after that!"

Cayden was frustrated. As far as he knew, he didn't do anything to her. How could he have? The last thing he remotely remembered was meeting John Smith from U.C.L.A. He pleaded in earnest. "I don't know what you mean, Emmaleigh! I don't know what you're talking about! I don't remember anything from tonight! I swear to God!"

"You liar! You 'swear to God' that you weren't over top of me, telling me you were going to 'take me to Heaven?'" This was news to Cayden. Michael balked, practically wretched, at the ridiculous phrase. It sounded like something Caemron would say.

Emmaleigh continued. "You 'swear to God' that you didn't say you were going to 'give me your staff?'" Michael, operating the last 14 hours on store-brand Pop Tarts, tasted them in his mouth a little.

"Emmaleigh," Cayden pleaded, "I swear it. I swear I didn't do that to you." Emmaleigh shook her head at him. Her memory of the night was fractured but she was certain that he was the villain. She cursed him and his behavior; Cayden continued to earnestly deny it.

It carried on like this for a while, but somehow Michael didn't hear a word of their exchange. It gently faded out until he heard only the hum of the pool filter, which became the dull ocean sound that one would find under the cover of sound-proof construction headphones. In this odd silence, Michael considered what was occurring before him. He saw their lips moving, but heard nothing. He saw her arms gesturing in accusation and Cayden's arms shifting in denial, but it all happened in slow motion.

As it transpired, he considered what was unraveling:
this was his opportunity to pry his crush away from
hers; he could bury Cayden, his rival, by corroborating
Emmaleigh's incomplete recollection of the night. "I
saw it, too, Emmaleigh," he could say, "You're right,
Cayden, you're a rapist and a scoundrel and only a MAC
caliber quarterback." All he would need to do is
corroborate the details she already knew to be true,
and subsequently he could achieve the culmination of
three years of secret pining. He watched tears finally
form in her eyes and weighed them against the pages of
notes written to himself, her name sketched in block
letters in the margins of his notebooks and then
furiously scribbled out, half-written emo songs with
purple lyrics all written in the same key... the
newspaper clippings she had taped inside her locker...

He could never do it to her.

Michael closed his eyes and readied himself to
sacrifice any attempt at ever winning his crush. The
sounds of the world came rushing back to him, like
waves cresting and crashing on rocks. Emmaleigh was
cursing Cayden; Cayden was still grasping at innocence.
The sharp words of their argument became audible again.
"I never want to see you again--" "Please listen to
me--" Etc. Etc.

"Stop!" Michael exclaimed, with more authority and
command than anyone had ever known him to have.

They both turned to him. Kody took a step backward
but still looked on in horrified fascination.

"Emmaleigh," he said, capturing both Cayden's and her attention, "Cayden wasn't the one who was trying to get on you." He sighed heavily. "I was. I was the one who brought you in here and I was the one who said," he paused, wishing he didn't have to accept responsibility for so cheesy a line, "I'm the one who said that I was going to give you--" He sighed. "I was going to give you--" He forced it. "I was going to give you my staff." The words came out like they tasted foul.

"What?" Cayden and Emmaleigh both exclaimed in accidental concert. Cayden was somewhat reassured but Emmaleigh just looked annoyed. Her memory of the night was fractured but this was latently inconsistent with it.

"Yeah, see, somebody spiked the punch and we were all tripping off of it, which explains why no one remembers anything. That's when I brought you in here to try to hook up with you. I wanted to make out and maybe get to second or third base," he paused, shrugged, and added, "I think. Isn't that the one where you get underneath the--?"

Emmaleigh's jaw gaped and Michael realized he was steering his false confession too far.

"But nothing happened!" he hastily reassured her. "Nothing happened! Before I could get to any bases, Cayden burst in here." He looked to Cayden with pretended admiration. "He burst in here to rescue you! And he said something like, 'I have to defend Emmaleigh's sacred womanly honor!'"

"He did?" They looked to Cayden. Cayden's face indicated that this was not familiar to him at all.

"Oh yeah. That's why he was over top of you. He was actually trying to, uh... resuscitate you." She looked cautiously toward Cayden, trying to gauge whether this was true.

"I could see how much he cared about you that it melted my icy heart and I promised to reform my ways," said Michael, feigning sincerity. He turned to Cayden and spoke solemnly.

"Thank you, Cayden. It took a real man to show me how to behave, uh, like a man. I guess that's tautological. But, you know. Thanks." But even Cayden wasn't convinced. He didn't remember picking up his date or applying her corsage or receiving his boutonnière or taking her to the auditorium, but he did remember hanging from the ten-meter platform, clinging to Michael, who had said something glib to him in a dead language before shaking him into the pool with unqualified vengeance.

"Why were you dangling me from the ten-meter board?"

Oh right. There was that. Michael frowned. "Well, before I reformed my ways, I decided to throw you in the pool."

"From the ten-meter platform?"

"That's right."

Cayden looked at him skeptically. Emmaleigh was already skeptical. "How'd you get up there?" she asked.

"I carried him."

"Thirty feet, directly up?"

Michael shrugged. "I'm strong."

There was a pause, a stand-off of sorts. Emmaleigh didn't remember the night well enough to be confident, but she somehow, someway knew it was a lie.

"His belt is over there," Emmaleigh protested to Michael, presenting it like evidence to the court, trying to convince him and reassure herself. "It's in the same place where I woke up."

Michael improvised. "I took it off of him to hit him with it. Same reason I threw him in the pool." Cayden checked himself for bruises. He had none.

"His shirt is off!" Emmaleigh protested.

Michael shrugged judgmentally. "It was an ugly shirt."

"Why are you saying this?" asked Emmaleigh.

"Why am I saying this? Because it's the truth! I was trying to get on you and Cayden stopped me!" He pointed to his friend for corroboration. "Ask Kody! He was watching the whole time!"

Everyone turned to Kody, who froze. Emmaleigh and Cayden didn't even realize he was there.

"Why were you 'watching the whole time'?" asked Cayden. "And what are you doing with that fire extinguisher?"

Kody mustered a long, uninspired "Uh..." and dropped the fire extinguisher to the ground. It made a heavy clang but fortunately did not crack the deck tile.

Cayden turned back to Michael. "How do you remember all of this if you drank this so-called spiked punch, too?"

Michael shrugged, getting annoyed with Cayden's and Emmaleigh's relentless attempt to learn an unfavorable truth. "I don't know. I guess it was me who spiked the punch. It was all part of my nefarious plan." He forced a sinister laugh. "Satisfied?"

"There was no punch," Emmaleigh recalled. Pieces of the night were slowly returning. They were not helping to corroborate Michael's grotesquely elaborate tale.

Michael grew frustrated and decided to skirt all the inconvenient verisimilitudes. "I drugged you all, okay! I just did. I used drugs to drug all of the people! I was feeling super rapey and I took everyone's shirts off! Jesus!"

She frowned at him skeptically, trying to figure him out, to turn over what he was hiding. There was a silent, momentary standoff that lasted six seconds but felt like a year. Cayden stood rigid, like a defendant awaiting an imminent verdict.

That's when Michael remembered the irrefutable proof concealed on his person.

"Emmaleigh, if it really was Cayden, then how am I the one who ended up with these?" He put his hands in his pocket and quickly produced a pair of red lacy underwear. Everyone paused and fixed on them, Kody especially. They were the type of underwear that would make most people blush. The kind that would horrify the fathers of daughters. The kind that no one would ever expect a guy like Michael to wave like a maritime flag.

They were Lucy's. A souvenir of sorts.

"No, that's not them." he said, stamping the drama from the reveal. "Just a sec," he continued. Fishing through his other pocket, he produced a second pair of panties and whipped them into view of the improvised court. These ones were white, plain, innocent, understated: they were Emmaleigh's. Kody took another step back and tried to turn himself invisible; Cayden's jaw dropped. Emmaleigh, too incredulous to believe what she had just witnessed, ran her hand down the small of her back to confirm that the undergarment was indeed missing from her body.

She had never, ever, ever, ever, ever, ever felt so humiliated or so violated.

With her left hand she snatched the understatedly sexy underwear from his grip and with her right hand she slapped him across the face harder than he would ever be slapped again.

The sound of it, a whip-crack like a jet breaking the sound barrier, echoed across the natatorium.

Dawn had broken 17 minutes & 33 seconds ago. The sun had washed away the orangish horizon that precedes the crisp mornings when summer bleeds into autumn. Emmaleigh and Cayden had both left the natatorium several minutes ago, together, as hero and heroine; Cayden to escort her to home & safety & the winter formal & bowling alleys & romantic fast food dine-ins & secret forbidden places afforded to them by parents who leave for the weekend & eventually into the Class Couple page of the senior mock elections, a page that would remain unautographed in Michael's copy come next spring.

Michael and Kody both sat together on the massive bleachers that had been installed for the spectators of school swim meets, Kody in confused, nervous awe of his friend and Michael in acute physical pain, blotting his raw ankle with a wet towel that perhaps only exacerbated the sting. He noticed the smell of the chlorinated air for the first time.

"Why didn't you tell them what really happened?" asked Kody, finally breaking the silence.

"What really happened? Sure." Michael turned to an invisible Emmaleigh and mocked himself aloud: "Hey Emmaleigh, *what really happened* was that Lucifer -- from the Bible -- possessed Cayden's body and attempted to use it to seduce you so that he could conquer the world per biblical prophesy, and I was obliged to save you after being duped by the janitor -- who by the way is an angel with a 150-watt flood light where his wang should be -- into serving you an adulterated Red Pop." He looked at Kody. "Would she believe that?" He paused. "I don't even believe it. Do you?"

Kody blinked. It did sound implausible that way.

"Besides, they're both stupid for each other. Why sabotage it for them?"

"Wow," said Kody. "You really are a good guy."

"I know," Michael said flatly. "It sucks."

A moment passed before Michael finally stood, testing his ankle and determining it was strong enough to limp on. "I think I'll stay home sick on Monday," he said.

"Probably a good idea," said Kody, also rising. "I've got to go find Jordyn." He started toward the door but hesitated. "Are you going to be okay?"

"Sure."

"What are you going to do now?"

Michael paused, haunted by memories of the night's
more lurid moments: Lucy pressing her cleavage against
him. Jessica's dress striking the floor. The student
teacher straddling him. Emmaleigh, once the love of his
life, making requests of him. "There's only one thing a
kid like me can do after a night like this," he said,
securing Lucy's lacy red underwear in his pocket. Kody
pretended to not fully understand what that meant. He
then walked across the cool tile floor and out of the
natatorium.

Michael, alone & un-sought & un-pursued for the
first time all night, walked to the door that exited to
the east athletic parking lot and threw it open. The
sun cast warm bright light onto his face. He squinted
and took a deep breath.

Exhaling, he glanced one last time over his shoulder
before limping out of the building and into the sun.
The heavy door to Crescent Lake High School fell behind
him with a heavy ka-chink.

Katie Van Pelt was the last student on campus at Crescent Lake. She sat on the cold concrete steps of the south entrance and gently weeped. She had turned down three invitations to the Homecoming dance and refused a reconciliation attempt from an affable ex-boyfriend while waiting & hoping for an invitation from the boy who sat two rows ahead in her AP English class. And, when it didn't happen and she had instead been forced to muster the courage to talk to him, he dismissed her with the most ridiculous of excuses. Trying to fight back a tear in her eye, she demanded toughness from herself. She would forget it. She would shrug off the burn of summary rejection. She would get over him.

Or maybe she would hold out for Prom.

TANTRIC INTERCOURSE

1	A	B	C	D		21	A	B	C	D		41	A	B
2	F	G	H	J		22	F	G	H	J		42	F	G
3	A	B	C	D		23	A	B	C	D		43	A	B
4	F	G	H	J		24	F	G	H	J		44	F	G
5	A	B	C	D		25	A	B	C	D		45	A	B
6	F	G	H	J		26	F	G	H	J		46	F	G
7	A	B	C	D		27	A	B	C	D		47	A	B
8	F	G	H	J		28	F	G	H	J		48	F	G
9	A	B	C	D		29	A	B	C	D		49	A	B
10	F	G	H	J		30	F	G	H	J		50	F	G
11	A	B	C	D		31	A	B	C	D		51	A	B
12	F	G	H	J		32	F	G	H	J		52	F	G
13	A	B	C	D		33	A	B	C	D		53	A	B
14	F	G	H	J		34	F	G	H	J		54	F	G
15	A	B	C	D		35	A	B	C	D		55	A	B
16	F	G	H	J		36	F	G	H	J		56	F	G
17	A	B	C	D		37	A	B	C	D		57	A	B
18	F	G	H	J		38	F	G	H	J		58	F	G
19	A	B	C	D		39	A	B	C	D		59	A	B
20	F	G	H	J		40	F	G	H	J		60	F	G

FALCONRY

1	A	B	C	D	E		16	F	G	H	J	K		31	A
2	F	G	H	J	K		17	A	B	C	D	E		32	F
3	A	B	C	D	E		18	F	G	H	J	K		33	A
4	F	G	H	J	K		19	A	B	C	D	E		34	F
5	A	B	C	D	E		20	F	G	H	J	K		35	A
6	F	G	H	J	K		21	A	B	C	D	E		36	F
7	A	B	C	D	E		22	F	G	H	J	K		37	A
8	F	G	H	J	K		23	A	B	C	D	E		38	F
9	A	B	C	D	E		24	F	G	H	J	K		39	A
10	F	G	H	J	K		25	A	B	C	D	E		40	F
11	A	B	C	D	E		26	F	G	H	J	K		41	A
12	F	G	H	J	K		27	A	B	C	D	E		42	F
13	A	B	C	D	E		28	F	G	H	J	K		43	A
14	F	G	H	J	K		29	A	B	C	D	E		44	F
15	A	B	C	D	E		30	F	G	H	J	K		45	A

About the Author

Matt Smith flunked out of the University of Michigan's College of Engineering and once resided in a parked Chevrolet on Ocean Park Boulevard. He now resides in suburban Detroit and spends his free time making oil paintings of bowls of fruit.

More at: MattFromTheHills.com